最直覺的英文文法

Useful
English Grammar

學習英文文法其實
Super Easy

讓你清晰完整的了解助動詞各種變化
所有必學且實用文法觀念盡收其中

國家圖書館出版品預行編目資料

最直覺的英文文法 / 潘威廉著. -- 初版.
-- 新北市 : 雅典文化, 民107.05印刷
面 ; 公分. -- (英語工具書 ; 16)
ISBN 978-986-96086-04-0 (18K平裝附光碟片)
1.英語 2.語法
805.16 107005134

英語工具書系列 16

最直覺的英文文法

執行編輯／潘紹傑
內文排版／王國卿
封面設計／姚恩涵

法律顧問：方圓法律事務所／涂成樞律師

總經銷：永續圖書有限公司
永續圖書線上購物網
www.foreverbooks.com.tw

CVS代理／美璟文化有限公司
TEL：（02）2723-9968
FAX：（02）2723-9668

出版日／2018年05月

雅典文化

出版社
22103 新北市汐止區大同路三段194號9樓之1
TEL （02）8647-3663
FAX （02）8647-3660

最直覺英文文法

對許多人來說，文法是英文中最難學的部分，有太多的規則。例如動詞可分成 be動詞和一般動詞，加上中文並沒有現在式、過去式、未來式的時態變化，讓很多人如同霧裡看花，越學越亂。

坊間一般文法書籍大致可分成兩種。第一種是以英文為母語的西方人士所寫的，這種文法書正確性最高，但不適合東方人學習，因為對西方人來說一切文法都是理所當然的，根本無法將心比心了解東方人對英文文法的疑惑在哪裡。

第二種是國人所寫，適合升學考試所用。這種文法書雖然是以中文為母語的華人角度為出發點，將英文文法濃縮成一些可記誦的規則，但與真實世界的英文頗有距離。

作者曾在美國求學、生活、工作，熟習最道地的美式英文文法，且有多年英文教學經驗，了解一般華人學習者的瓶頸何在。因此本書將重點放在最關鍵、最常用句型，讓讀者以直覺及由淺入深的方式透過不斷練習即可使用正確英文，並透過舉一反三的方式，讓人了解英文文法中的基本觀念。

本書的定位為初階到中階都適用，不會要求讀者背誦一大堆的文法規則。事實上若靠記憶文法規則學英文，也是違反人類學習語言的本能。不論是聽說讀寫，讀者只要照著本書練習即可應付大部分的場合。

任何一種語言都會隨著時間改變，英文也是如此（尤其是假設語氣與助動詞等），因此本書將整理出最通用且不隨時間改變的文法，讓讀者可以少走冤枉路，避免學到已經過時或罕見的文法。

序言

1. 最基本句型 011

2. 動詞基本觀念 027

Part 1

最基本句型

• 主詞 + be 動詞 + 冠詞 + 名詞

例 I am a student.
我是一個學生。

例 You are a teacher.
你是一位老師。

例 He is a doctor.
他是一位醫生。

例 She is a cook.
她是一位廚師。

例 John is a cop.
約翰是一位警察。

習慣上句子第一個字的第一個字母要大寫，如I, You, He, She....

上面三句中“我、你、他”就是主詞，表示句子的主角。這三句和中文的用法幾乎完全相同，唯一不同處是我、你、他的 be 動詞 (am, are, is)都不一樣。

所謂 be 動詞通常就是中文的“是”。

例 We are students.
我們是學生。(we are可簡寫成we're)

例 You are teachers.

你們是老師。

例 They are singers.
他們是歌星。

例 Joe and Tom are actors.
喬和湯姆是演員。

英文中有單數、複數的差別，單數就是一個、複數是一個以上。

名詞複數時就不用冠詞a，但後面要加s。(students, teachers, singers , actors前面都沒有a，但後面多了s)。

例 Kent and Mary are husband and wife.
肯特和瑪莉是夫妻。(一夫和一妻所以husband 和 wife後面沒加s)

例 You and I are friends.
你和我是朋友。

例 She and he are teachers.
她和他是老師。

be動詞變化表			
單數	第一人稱	**I** (我， 一定要大寫)	**am**
	第二人稱	**you** (你或妳)	**are**
	第三人稱	**he** (他)	**is**
		she (她)	**is**
		it (它----除了人以外包括動物)	**is**
		除了**I**和**you**以外單獨的人、事、物	**is**
複數	第一人稱	**we** (我們)	**are**
	第二人稱	**you** (你們或妳們)	**are**
	第三人稱	**they** (他們、她們、它們)	**are**
		除了**we**和**you**以外，一個以上的人、事、物	**are**

主詞是單數時I用am，you用are，其他情況都用is，主詞是複數時be動詞都用are。

有一個術語不妨牢記: 我和我們是第一人稱。
你和你們是第二人稱。其餘都是第三人稱。
我,你,他→1,2,3， 其實蠻好記的。

1. 你是商人。
2. Sandy是護士。
3. Mike 和 Donald 是朋友。
4. 它們是貓和狗。
5. 他們是計程車司機。
6. Cindy和我是美國人。

1. You are a businessman.

   說明：你是單數，所以要加上a。

2. Sandy is a nurse.

   說明：只有一個人用is。

3. Mike and Donald are friends.
4. They are cats and dogs.
5. They are taxi drivers.
6. Cindy and I are Americans.

   說明：雖然不在句首，I 還是要大寫。

主詞 + be 動詞 + 形容詞

顧名思義形容詞就是用來形容人或事物的字，例如:美麗的、可愛的、大的等等。

例 She is beautiful.
她是漂亮的。

例 Dogs are faithful.
狗是忠實的。

例 They are cute.
他們是可愛的。

例 I am happy.
我是快樂的。

例 Water is important.
水是重要的。

例 He is tall and thin.
他高且瘦。

例 She is young and smart.
她年輕聰明

例 It is black and white.
它是黑白的。

主詞 + be 動詞 + （冠詞） + 形容詞 + 名詞

例 I am a happy person.
我是一個快樂的人。

例 Dogs are faithful animals.
狗是忠實的動物。

例 She is a beautiful woman.
她是一個美麗的女人。

例 They are beautiful flowers.
他們是美麗的花。

例 Joseph and Jon are good friends.
約瑟和瓊是好朋友。

就和前面提到的一樣，單數時名詞前面要加a，複數時字尾加s。

否定句的用法

這點英文和中文不同，中文說不是，英文卻是將not (不)放在be動詞後面。

例 I'm not a girl.
我不是一個女孩。(I'm是I am 的簡寫)

例 It's not funny.
這不好笑。(It's 是It is的簡寫)

例 This is not a book.
這不是一本書。

例 That flower isn't blue.
那朵花不是藍色的。(isn't 是 is not的簡寫)

例 They're not trees.
它們不是樹。(they're是 they are的簡寫)

This	這	單數
that	那	單數
these	這些	複數
those	那些	複數

★其他簡寫

例 That's not me.
那不是我。(that's 是that is的簡寫)

注意：this is不可簡寫成this's。

例 She's pretty.
她漂亮。(She's 是She is的簡寫)

例 He's my lawyer.
他是我的律師。(He's 是He is的簡寫)

例 You're not my mother.
你不是我的母親。(You're是 You are的簡寫)

例 They aren't Americans.
他們不是美國人。

例 We aren't soldiers.
我們不是士兵。

例 It's not free.
它不是免費的。

疑問句的使用

問對方問題時要將be動詞放在主詞前面。

例 Are you Jessica?
妳是潔西卡嗎？

例 Am I angry?
我生氣嗎？

例 Is his car white?
他的車是白色的嗎？

例 Are they Taiwanese?
他們是台灣人嗎？

Yes, they are Taiwanese.
是的，他們是台灣人。(肯定回答，也可只說：Yes, they are.)

No, they are not Taiwanese.
不，他們不是台灣人。(否定回答，也可只說：No, they are not.)

疑問句和否定句同時使用

例 Am I not pretty?
我不漂亮嗎？

例 Aren't they adorable?
他們不可愛嗎？ (aren't 是 are not的簡寫)

例 Aren't you tired?
妳不累嗎？ (這種說法比Are you not tired? 更常見)

例 Isn't Tim a nice guy?
難道Tim不是好人嗎？(這句英文的意思就是: Tim 真是個好人!大多數情況下人們會習慣這樣用，而不說：Is Tim not a nice guy?)

例 Isn't it cool?
它不酷嗎？ (這句英文的意思就是: 它真酷！)

注意：上面例句可看到be動詞移到句首。若be動詞和not合在一起簡寫時（如：**aren't, isn't**）也是移到句首。但如果be動詞和not沒有合在一起簡寫時，**not**還是放在主詞後面。例如：**Isn't is cool? = Is it not cool?**

<table>
<tr><th colspan="3">所有格變化表</th></tr>
<tr><td rowspan="5">單數</td><td>第一人稱</td><td>my (我的)</td></tr>
<tr><td>第二人稱</td><td>your (你的或妳的)</td></tr>
<tr><td rowspan="3">第三人稱</td><td>his (他的)</td></tr>
<tr><td>her (她的)</td></tr>
<tr><td>its (它的)</td></tr>
<tr><td rowspan="3">複數</td><td>第一人稱</td><td>our (我們的)</td></tr>
<tr><td>第二人稱</td><td>your (你們的或妳們的)</td></tr>
<tr><td>第三人稱</td><td>their (他們的、她們的、它們的)</td></tr>
</table>

例 This is my pet.
這是我的寵物。

例 Your house is very large.
你的房子很大。

例 Is her name Judy?
她的名字是Judy嗎？

例 He is my father.
他是我的父親。

例 He is not our President.
他不是我們的總統。

例 Aren't you their friends?
你不是他們的朋友嗎？

例 Its eyes are very big.
它的眼睛很大。(它有兩個眼睛，所以用eyes和are。)

注意：**It's not my book. = It isn't my book. = It is not my book.**

例 It is his hat.
這是他的帽子。

例 I have a horse. Its name is Winner.
我有一匹馬。它的名子是Winner。

例 Are they your moms?
她們是你們的媽媽？

注意：由於媽媽用複數，所以這裡的**your**應該是「你們的」。

請在(a) (b) (c) (d)中選出正確答案（可能是複選）

1. Sabrina ______ a dancer.

   (a) not is (b) is not (c) are not (d) not are

2. I _____ a student.

   (a) is (b) are (c) am (d) amn't

3. Its legs ____ very long.

   (a) is (b) are (c) am (d) arent

4. ____ you happy?

   (a) is (b) are (c) am (d) Are

5. ____ John a Taiwanese?

   (a) Isn't (b) Isnt (c) Am not (d) Aren't

6. ____ eyes are big.

   (a) Its (b) It's (c) You're (d) We

7. Mary is ____.

   (a) sad (b) a sad man (c) a sad woman (d) sad girl

8. Those ____ are red.

   (a) flower (b) table (c) chair (d) desks

9. ____ name is Michael.

   (a) Her (b) His (c) Their (d) Our

10. This ____ a joke.

    (a) is (b) is not (c) are (d) am

1. (b) Sabrina是一個人名，用單數。not放在be動詞後面。

2. (c) I後面的be動詞一定用am。否定句時用am not，沒有amn't這個字。

3. (b) legs是複數，要用are。否定句簡寫是aren't，沒有arent這個字。

4. (d) you的be動詞是are，因為放在句首所以A要大寫。

5. (a) John是第三人稱單數，要用isn't，isnt是錯誤拼法。

6. (a) Its：它的。

7. (a) (c) Mary是女性名，不可用(b) ，(d) 少了冠詞a。

8. (d) Those是那些，所以後面接複數。

9. (b) Michael是男性第三人稱單數。

10. (a) (b) This後面接單數is或is not，所以(a) (b)都對。

Part 2

動詞基本觀念

前面介紹過be動詞，現在介紹一般動詞。一般動詞代表動作，例如walk (走路)、sing (唱歌)、eat (吃飯)等。另外有些一般動詞可表示一種狀態，例如：exist (存在)、stand (站)。

與be動詞一樣，一般動詞也有肯定句、否定句、疑問句三種。肯定句——主詞是第三人稱單數時，動詞後面要加s

I play guitar. You play guitar. We play guitar. (動詞play後面都沒加s)

He plays guitar. She plays guitar. Zach plays guitar. (動詞play後面都加s)

否定句時，當主詞不是第三人稱單數時，動詞前面加do not。

I do not work. You do not work. We do not work. They do not work.

主詞是第三人稱單數時，動詞前面加does not。

He does not work. She does not work. It does not work. Michael does not work.

注意：**does not**後面動詞改用原型，也就是動詞不加**s**。
do not可簡寫成**don't**。**does not** 可簡寫成**doesn't**。

You don't work. Jane doesn't work.

Do和does是助動詞，我們以後會再詳細討論。

注意：前面教過**be**動詞的否定句是將**not**放在**be**動詞後面。例如：**He is not a student.**
然而一般動詞的否定句卻是將**do not**或**does not**放在動詞前面。

疑問句時，當主詞不是第三人稱單數時，動詞前面加do。
當主詞是第三人稱單數時，動詞前面加does。

Do I work?	非第三人稱單數用**do**
Do you work?	非第三人稱單數用**do**
Do we work?	非第三人稱單數用**do**
Do they work?	非第三人稱單數用**do**
Does he work?	第三人稱單數用**does**
Does she work?	第三人稱單數用**does**
Does it work?	第三人稱單數用**does**
Does Michael work?	第三人稱單數用**does**

Ⓐ Do you like sushi? (你喜歡壽司嗎？)

Ⓑ Yes, I like sushi. (是的，我喜歡壽司。)

注意：上面回答可改成**Yes, I do.** 用**do**來取代**like sushi**，如此可簡化回答。如果**B**回答：**No, I don't like sushi.** (不，我不喜歡壽司。)——則可簡化成：**No, I don't.**

Ⓐ Does Mike play violin? (麥可拉小提琴嗎？)

Ⓑ Yes, he plays violin. (是的，麥可拉小提琴。)

或者簡化成Yes, he does (是的，他拉。)或 No he doesn't. (不，他不拉。)

Ⓐ Your grandmother looks so energetic. (你的祖母看起來如此精力充沛。)

Ⓑ Yes, she does. (是的，她是。)

Ⓐ I think Jack lives in Sweden. (我想傑克在瑞典居住。)

Ⓑ No he doesn't. (不，他不是。)

再次強調！！！

當主詞是第三人稱單數時，否定句或疑問句的動詞都沒加s。因為助動詞後面的動詞都不用加s。

Helen knows Susan. (✓)

Helen doesn't knows Susan. (✕)

Jack doesn't know Susan. (✓)

Jack don't know Susan. (✕)...第三人稱單數用doesn't

一般說來，主詞是第三人稱單數時，動詞後面要加s，這是所謂的規則變化。但也有不規則變化，例如：當動詞字尾是 s, x, z, -sh, -ch, 的時候，字尾加 es。

動詞	主詞是第三人稱單數	中文	動詞	主詞是第三人稱單數	中文
pass	**passes**	經過	**finish**	**finishes**	完成
miss	**misses**	想念	**push**	**pushes**	推
fix	**fixes**	修理	**hatch**	**hatches**	孵
buzz	**buzzes**	響	**teach**	**teaches**	教

例 He teaches me English.
他教我英文。

例 John fixes the problem.
約翰解決了這個問題。

當動詞字尾是子音 + y的時候，字尾要去 y 加上 ies

動詞	主詞是第三人稱單數
fly	**flies**
cry	**cries**
study	**studies**
marry	**marries**

例 I study German.
我讀德文。

例 Sabrina studies German.
薩賓娜讀德文。

例 They cry.
他們哭。

例 She cries.
她哭。

特殊情形

動詞	主詞是第三人稱單數
go	**goes**
do	**does**

例 Something goes wrong (✓)
Something gos wrong (×)
有些事出錯。

例 He does not speak French. (✓)
He dos not speak French. (×)
他不說法文。

現在式

到目前為止我們前面用的都是現在式，現在式表示現在如此或固定會做的事。
現在式時，主詞是第三人稱單數，一般動詞後面要加s，be動詞有am, is, are的區分。正如同我們前面提過的。

例 I'm nineteen years old.
我現在十九歲。(現在如此)

例 Jackson does not play soccer.
傑克遜不踢足球。(現在如此)

例 Does she drive to work every morning?
她每天早晨開車上班嗎？ (固定會做的事)

例 Sunny visits her parents every weekend.
Sunny每週末都探望她的父母。(固定會做的事)

現在式也可表示現在或未來行程已經安排好的事情

例 The school term starts next week.
學期從下週開始。

例 The train leaves at 7pm this evening.
火車在今晚七點離開。

例 We have a lesson next Monday.
我們下星期一有一堂課。

現在式也可表示自然界固定發生的現象，或不會改變的事。

例 Water freezes at zero degrees.
水在零度結冰。

例 The earth circles the sun.
地球環繞太陽。

例 Her mother is a Japanese.
她的母親是日本人。

例 The Nile flows through Egypt.
尼羅河流經埃及。

例 The sun rises in the east.
太陽從東邊升起。

例 We are humans.
我們是人類。

例 Everest is the highest mountain.
珠穆朗瑪峰是最高的山峰。

動詞三態

動詞三態是指原形動詞、過去式、過去分詞。
一般動詞的現在式就是用原形動詞，若主詞是第三人稱單數，原形一般動詞後面要加s。
至於be動詞 (am, is are)的原形動詞是be。
大部份的動詞三態都是規則變化，過去式和過去分詞相同，直接在原形動詞後面加ed。
現在式用原形動詞，那過去式和過去分詞用在什麼地方？我們馬上會提到。

過去式和過去分詞相同，直接在原形動詞後面加**ed**。字尾是無聲子音，**ed**唸**[t]**			
原形動詞	過去式	過去分詞	中文
like	**liked**	**liked**	喜歡
pick	**picked**	**picked**	挑選
laugh	**laughed**	**laughed**	大笑
wash	**washed**	**washed**	洗
book	**booked**	**booked**	訂房
work	**worked**	**worked**	工作
watch	**watched**	**watched**	看
miss	**missed**	**missed**	思念
develop	**developed**	**developed**	發展

字尾是有聲子音ed唸[d]			
原形動詞	過去式	過去分詞	中文
harm	**harmed**	**harmed**	傷害
live	**lived**	**lived**	住
repair	**repaired**	**repaired**	修理
offer	**offered**	**offered**	提供
ruin	**ruined**	**ruined**	毀壞

字尾是母音ed唸[d]			
原形動詞	過去式	過去分詞	中文
play	**played**	**played**	玩
snow	**snowed**	**snowed**	下雪
circle	**circled**	**circled**	圍圓圈
stay	**stayed**	**stayed**	停留

字尾是d或t時ed唸[Id]			
原形動詞	過去式	過去分詞	中文
visit	**visited**	**visited**	訪問
paint	**painted**	**painted**	畫
end	**ended**	**ended**	結束
want	**wanted**	**wanted**	想要

字尾是**e**直接加**d**			
原形動詞	過去式	過去分詞	中文
amaze	**amazed**	**amazed**	使驚訝
agree	**agreed**	**agreed**	同意
bake	**baked**	**baked**	烘培

下列字過去式、過去分詞要重複字尾，再加**ed**。			
原形動詞	過去式	過去分詞	中文
travel	**travelled**	**travelled**	旅行
admit	**admitted**	**admitted**	承認
occur	**occurred**	**occurred**	發生
refer	**referred**	**referred**	參考
prefer	**preferred**	**preferred**	較喜歡
transfer	**transferred**	**transferred**	移動
control	**controlled**	**controlled**	控制
beg	**begged**	**begged**	請求
fit	**fitted**	**fitted**	適合
plan	**planned**	**planned**	計畫
drop	**dropped**	**dropped**	落下
stop	**stopped**	**stopped**	停止
skip	**skipped**	**skipped**	跳
cancel	**cancelled**	**cancelled**	取消

字尾是子音+y時，過去式和過去分詞為去y加**ied**，發音加上**[d]**。			
原形動詞	過去式	過去分詞	中文
study	**studied**	**studied**	讀書
satisfy	**satisfied**	**satisfied**	滿足
cry	**cried**	**cried**	哭
try	**tried**	**tried**	嘗試
carry	**carried**	**carried**	攜帶
marry	**married**	**married**	結婚

下列兩個字過去式和過去分詞加**ked**，發音加上**[t]**。			
原形動詞	過去式	過去分詞	中文
panic	**panicked**	**panicked**	恐慌
picnic	**picnicked**	**picnicked**	野餐

所有跟科技有關的新字都是規則變化			
原形動詞	過去式	過去分詞	中文
fax	**faxed**	**faxed**	傳真
email	**emailed**	**emailed**	寄電郵
google	**googled**	**googled**	搜尋

現在開始介紹不規則變化的動詞三態

三態同形 (AAA)			
動詞原形	過去式	過去分詞	中文
cut	**cut**	**cut**	割
cost	**cost**	**cost**	值
hit	**hit**	**hit**	打
hurt	**hurt**	**hurt**	傷害
let	**let**	**let**	讓
read	**read**	**read**	讀
set	**set**	**set**	放置

過去分詞和動詞原形同形（ABA）			
動詞原形	過去式	過去分詞	中文
become	**became**	**become**	變成
come	**came**	**come**	來
run	**ran**	**run**	跑

過去式和過去分詞同形（ABB）			
動詞原形	過去式	過去分詞	中文
bring	**brought**	**brought**	帶來
build	**built**	**built**	建造
buy	**bought**	**bought**	買
catch	**caught**	**caught**	捕捉
dig	**dug**	**dug**	挖
feed	**fed**	**fed**	餵
feel	**felt**	**felt**	感覺
fight	**fought**	**fought**	戰鬥
find	**found**	**found**	發現
flee	**fled**	**fled**	逃跑
get	**got**	**got**	得到
hang	**hung**	**hung**	吊
have	**had**	**had**	有
hear	**heard**	**heard**	聽
hold	**held**	**held**	把握
keep	**kept**	**kept**	保持
lay	**laid**	**laid**	放
lead	**led**	**led**	帶領
leave	**left**	**left**	離開
light	**lit**	**lit**	點燃

lose	lost	lost	失去
make	made	made	做
meet	met	met	遇見
pay	paid	paid	付
say	said	said	說
sell	sold	sold	賣
send	sent	sent	送
sit	sat	sat	坐
sleep	slept	slept	睡
spend	spent	spent	花費
stand	stood	stood	站
teach	taught	taught	教
tell	told	told	告訴
think	thought	thought	想
understand	understood	understood	了解

三態不同形（ABC）			
動詞原形	過去式	過去分詞	中文
be (am, are, is)	**was、were**	**been**	**be**動詞
do	**did**	**done**	做
go	**went**	**gone**	去
sew	**sewed**	**sewn**	縫
show	**showed**	**shown**	展示
begin	**began**	**begun**	開始
drink	**drank**	**drunk**	喝
ring	**rang**	**rung**	電話響
sing	**sang**	**sung**	唱
sink	**sank**	**sunk**	沉
swim	**swam**	**swum**	游泳
bear	**bore**	**born**	忍受
tear	**tore**	**torn**	撕
wear	**wore**	**worn**	穿
blow	**blew**	**blown**	吹
draw	**drew**	**drawn**	畫
fly	**flew**	**flown**	飛
grow	**grew**	**grown**	生長
know	**knew**	**known**	知道
throw	**threw**	**thrown**	丟
break	**broke**	**broken**	打破
choose	**chose**	**chosen**	選擇
eat	**ate**	**eaten**	吃
fall	**fell**	**fallen**	掉
forget	**forgot**	**forgotten**	忘記
give	**gave**	**given**	給

rise	rose	risen	升起
see	saw	seen	看
shake	shook	shaken	搖
speak	spoke	spoken	說
steal	stole	stolen	偷
bite	bit	bitten	咬
drive	drove	driven	開車
hide	hid	hidden	躲
ride	rode	ridden	騎
take	took	taken	拿
wake	woke	woken	叫醒
write	wrote	written	寫

：動詞三態規則變化不須額外記憶，過去式和過去分詞只要在動詞後面加**ed**就好。不規則變化的部分需要讀者花點時間牢記。

過去式

過去式表示以前曾經如此，但現在並非如此的狀態。

Be動詞部分，單數主詞 (除了you)都用was，複數主詞都用were，you不管單複數都用were。

肯定句	否定句	疑問句
I was a lawyer.	**I was not a lawyer.**	**Was I a lawyer?**
He was in London in 1999.	**He was not in London in 1999.**	**Was he in London in 1999?**
She was my girlfriend.	**She was not my girlfriend.**	**Was she my girlfriend?**
It was a parrot.	**It was not a parrot.**	**Was it a parrot?**
You were a student.	**You were not a student.**	**Were you a student?**
You were students.	**You were not students.**	**Were you students?**
We were together.	**We were not together.**	**Were we together?**
They were funny.	**They were not funny.**	**Were they funny?**

was not 可縮寫成 wasn't，were not可縮寫成weren't。

It was not a cat. = It wasn't a cat.

We were not home = We weren't home.

一般動詞過去式，即使是第三人稱單數也不用加s，這點和現在式不同。

He takes this class. (現在式第三人稱單數動詞加s)

We take this class.

He took this class. (過去式不管主詞是第幾人稱動詞都不加s)

We took this class.

否定句在動詞前面加did not，Did後面動詞變回原形。

didn't可縮寫成did not

He went home last night.

He didn't go home last night. (動詞變回原形go)

I saw you yesterday.

I didn't see you yesterday. (動詞變回原形see)

We had a helicopter last year.

We didn't have a helicopter last year. (動詞變回原形 have)

疑問句把did或didn't放在句子最前面。Did後面動詞變回原形

例 I owned an iPhone.
我有一個iPhone。

例 Did you own an iPhone?
你有iPhone嗎？

例 Yes, I owned an iPhone.
是的，我有一個iPhone。(肯定回答)

例 No, I didn't own an iPhone.
不，我沒有iPhone。(否定回答)

例 Didn't you own an iPhone?
你沒有iPhone嗎？

過去式可用在表示按先後順序

例 Linda watered the garden, took a shower, and then went to bed.
琳達在花園澆水，洗澡，然後上床睡覺。

used to 加動詞原形，用在過去式

例 Some people used to call him an idiot.
有些人以前叫他白痴。

例 David didn't use to live in Canada.
大衛以前沒住在加拿大。

例 Did you use to exercise regularly?
你以前是否定期運動？

注意：be動詞+ used to + 動名詞或名詞...表示習慣於做某事，不同於上面提到的used to + 動詞。
所謂動名詞就是原形動詞 + ing，後面會再討論。

例 I'm used to living on my own. (現在式)
我習慣於自己生活

例 Tammy is used to working night shift. (現在式)
Tammy習慣於上夜班。

例 They weren't used to the hot weather. (過去式)
他們不習慣炎熱的天氣。

及物動詞與不及物動詞

動詞可分成及物與不及物兩種，前者表示動詞的動作與後面的字有關。

例 She speaks English.
她說英語。(動詞speaks和English有關)

例 We visit him.
我們拜訪他。(動詞visit和him有關)

例 Please sing a song.
請唱一首歌。(動詞sing和a song有關)

上面例子中動詞後面的字承受了動詞的動作，所以稱為受詞。
前面曾提過代名詞主格，現在來看受格。

代名詞受格變化表		
單數	第一人稱	**me** (我)
	第二人稱	**you** (你或妳)
	第三人稱	**him** (他)
		Her (她)
		It (它)
複數	第一人稱	**us** (我們)
	第二人稱	**you** (你們或妳們)
	第三人稱	**them** (他們、她們、它們)

We visit they. (✕) (動詞後面要接受格)

We visit them. (✓)

Them visit us. (✕) (動詞前面要用主格)

They visit us. (✓)

不及物動詞後面沒有受詞

例 It falls.
它掉落。

例 They run.
他們跑。

例 She smiles.
她微笑。

有些情況下及物動詞後面有兩個受詞，下列兩種用法都可以。

例 My wife sent me an email. (✓)
我的妻子寄給我一封電子郵件。(me放在動詞後面)

例 My wife sent an email to me. (✓)
我的妻子寄一封電子郵件給我。(an email放在動詞後面)

to是介係詞，表示：到…

例 Run to me.
請跑到我這裡。

例 He bought his mother some flowers. (✓)
He bought some flowers for his mother. (✓)
他為他的母親買了一些花。

for是介係詞，表示：為了…

有些動詞同時是及物動詞與不及物動詞。

例 A bird sings. (不及物動詞後面不接受詞)
一隻鳥歌唱。

例 Please sing a song. (及物動詞後面接受詞a song)
請唱一首歌。

例 He opened the door. (及物動詞)
他打開門。

例 The museum opens at 11 o'clock. (不及物動詞)
博物館11點開門。

主動式/被動式

到目前為止我們都是用主動式，現在開始介紹被動式。動詞的被動用法以 be 動詞加上過去分詞表示。其中，be 動詞要依照時態不同而改變。

例 Tim cleans the window every morning.（主動式）
Tim每天早上都清潔窗戶。

例 The window is cleaned by Tim every morning. (被動式)
窗戶每天早上都被Tim清潔。(介係詞by表示被某人完成)

cleans後面加s，表示現在式，所以被動式要用is cleaned。

例 Tom repaired the car.（主動式）
湯姆修理這輛汽車。

例 The car was repaired by Tom.（被動式)
這輛汽車是湯姆修理的。

repair 後面加ed，表示過去式，所以被動式要用was repaired。Repair的過去式和過去分詞都是repaired。

例 Nancy sent a flower to me. (主動式)
南希送我一朵花。(這句中sent是過去式)

例 A flower was sent to me by Nancy. (被動式)
一朵花被南希送給我。(這句中sent是過去分詞)

例 I was sent a flower by Nancy. (被動式)
我被南希送了一朵花。(這句中sent是過去分詞)

上面兩句被動式在中文看起來怪怪的，英文文法卻是正確的。Send (送)的三態變化是send/sent/sent，過去式和過去分詞同型。

被動用法常使用在不知是誰做的事，或誰做的不是重點的情形。

例 Her car was stolen.
他車被偷了。(不知是誰偷的)

例 English is spoken all over the world.
英文在世界各地都有人說。(哪些人說英文不是重點)

例 564 babies were born in this hospital in 2015.
2015年564名嬰兒出生在這家醫院。(嬰兒被哪些母親生的不是重點)

例 A company in Taiwan made this product. (主動式)
台灣的一家公司做了這個產品。

This product was made in Taiwan. (被動式)
這產品是在台灣製造的。(哪家公司製造的不是重點，重點是台灣貨。)

有些動詞是不及物動詞，因此沒有被動式。

例 She cried.
她哭了。

例 The sun rises.
太陽升起。

例 People come and go.
人們來來去去。

例 We smiled.
我們笑了。

例 We laugh every day.
我們每天都笑。

例 They frowned.
他們皺著眉頭。

使役動詞

特性：後面一定接原型動詞

Let...讓

例 Johnson let me drive his BWV.
強森讓我駕駛他的BWV。

例 Janet let her son goes fishing. (✕)
Janet let her son go fishing. (✓) (her son雖然是第三人稱單數，let 後面go用原型。)
珍妮特讓她的兒子去釣魚。

Make... 強迫某人做某事

例 Our coach made us do 50 situps.
我們教練強迫我們做50個仰臥起坐。

例 Geena made her children do their homework.
吉娜強迫她的孩子做功課。

Have...讓人覺得有義務做某事

例 I had Quincy fix my roof.
我讓昆西修復我的屋頂。

例 I had the mechanic check my brakes.
我讓機械師檢查我的剎車。

祈使句

英文中的祈使句不加主詞，表示希望對方做某件事，而且一定用原型動詞。

1. Hurry up!快點！
2. Do not smoke!不要抽菸！
3. Never give up!絕不要放棄！
4. Turn left.向左轉。
5. Have a seat.坐下。
6. Do be quiet.一定要安靜。

Do放在動詞前面表示：一定或真的。

例 I do love you.
我真的愛妳。

動詞片語

動詞片語就是動詞 ＋ 介係詞或副詞
動詞片語通常用在口語上的表達，在正式文章中較少使用。
動詞片語通常和原來動詞意義不同。

例 My baby Jonah can count to 30.
我的寶貝約拿可以數到30。(count：數)

例 I can count on you.
我可以依靠你。(count on是依靠，意義與count完全不同)

例 George put his wallet on the table.
喬治把他的錢包放在桌子上。(put：放)

例 Tina put on her jacket.
蒂娜穿上她的外套。(put on：穿上)

例 They put off the meeting.
他們延後了會議。(put off：延後)

例 I want to get a master degree.
我想獲得碩士學位。(get：得到)

例 Get on the bus now!
現在上公車吧！ (get on：上車)

例 Brian usually gets off the bus at this stop.
布萊恩通常在這站下車。(get off：下車)

例 Muslims don't eat pork.
穆斯林不吃豬肉。(eat：吃)

例 I seldom eat out.
我很少吃外面。(eat out：在外吃飯)

例 He can eat everything up.
他可以吃完每樣食物。(eat up：吃完)

如果動詞後面受詞是代名詞時，通常將代名詞放在動詞片語中間，而非後面。

Write down the sentence. (✓)

Write the sentence down. (✓) (名詞可放在動詞片語中間或後面)

例 Write it down. (✓) (代名詞可放在動詞片語中間)
Write down it. (✕) (代名詞不可放在動詞片語後面)
寫下這句子。

例 Switch the light off. (✓)
Switch off the light. (✓)
Switch it off. (✓)
Switch off it. (✕)
關燈。

請在(a) (b) (c) (d)中選出正確答案（可能是複選）

1. Sara and Eve ____ work.

   (a) do not (b) does not (c) don't (d) dont

2. Do ____ work?

   (a) she (b) you (c) Tom (d) Tom and Helen

3. A: Do you like apple juice?

   B: Yes! I ____.

   (a) like apple juice (b) do (c) don't (d) am

4. Susan ____ Jack.

   (a) know (b) knows (c) don't know (d) doesn't know

5. John ____ him French.

   (a) teach (b) teachs (c) teaches (d) doesn't teaches

6. He ____home last night.

   (a) went (b) didn't went (c) didn't go (d) wasn't go

7. I had my son ____ his homework.

   (a) does (b) do (c) did (d) didn't

8. Tammy visited ____.

   (a) Wilson (b) he (c) him (d) us

9. Lisa ____ the swimming class.

   (a) took (b) tooks (c) tooked (d) take

10. ____ you play golf?

    (a) Do (b) Did (c) Are (d) Were

1. (a) (c) 主詞是兩個人，為複數。一般動詞否定句前面加do not或don't。
2. (b) (d) 除了第三人稱單數以外，一般動詞疑問句前面加do。
3. (a) (b) (a) 是完整回答，(b) 是簡答。
4. (b) (d) Susan是第三人稱單數，肯定句know後面加s，否定句前面加doesn't。
5. (c) teach在第三人稱單數時，後面加es。
6. (a) (c) didn't後面接原形go，不接went。
7. (b) 使役動詞後面接原形動詞do。
8. (a) (c) (d) 一般動詞後面接名詞或代名詞受格。
9. (a) took是過去式，後面不加s或ed。(d) 錯在take後面沒加s。
10. (a) (b) play是一般動詞，前面可用do或did。

Part 3

冠詞

第一章提到過a是一個冠詞，意思是：一個，放在單數名詞的前面，例如：a book (一本書)，a computer (一台電腦)等。
事實上a是放在第一個字母是子音的名詞前。但如果名詞第一個字母是母音的話就不用a，而改用an。
子音、母音如何區分？a, e, i, o, u就是母音，其他都是子音。

a (名詞第一個字母是子音)	**an** (名詞第一個字母是母音… **a, e, i, o, u)**
a town	**an umbrella**
a pen	**an apple**
a bird	**an eagle**
a ticket	**an iPad**
a dancer	**an office**

例外	
字母開頭是子音，發音卻為母音，要用**an**	字母開頭是母音，發音卻為子音，要用**a**
an hour	**a Euro**
an honer	**a one-day pass**
an FBI agent	**a university**

a 和 an是指一個，所以不可以放在複數名詞前面

A books. (✕)

A book. (✓)

如果名詞前面有形容詞，則要看形容詞第一個字母是母音或子音來決定用a 或 an

An excellent student

A nice try

不可數名詞前面不加a 或 an，可數名詞前面要加a 或 an

例 A horse is an animal. (✓)
A horse is animal. (✕)
馬是動物。

例 I need money. (✓)
I need a money. (✕)
我需要錢。
錢是不可數，所以前面不加a，但如果是dollar (元)就可數，可以說I need a dollar.

除了a與an外，另有一個冠詞是the，the也稱為「定冠詞」，它也是放在名詞前面，不同之處在於the是專指特定的人、事、物、地。

例 I am a father.
我是一個父親。

例 I am the father of Joseph.
我就是喬瑟夫的父親。

例 I saw a bright star.
我看到一顆明亮的星星。(天上星星有很多顆，其中一顆是明亮的)

例 It is the bright star.
它是這顆明亮的星星。(專指明亮的這顆，其他星星都不亮)

例 The CEO of IBM is here.
IBM的執行長在這裡。

例 I have a cat. The cat is black.
我有一隻貓。這隻是黑色的。

日、月、世界、天空前面要加the

例 The sun and the moon are bright.
太陽和月亮是明亮的。

例 We bless all the children in the world.
我們祝福世界上所有的小孩。

例 I saw a cloud in the sky.
我在天空中看到一片雲。

The + 西元（一定是10的倍數）+ 's表示某年代

例 He was born in the 1970's.
他出生於1970年代。

例 We miss the days in the 1980's.
我們懷念1980年代的日子。

the + 名字 + s表示某某家族。

The Obamas (歐巴馬家族), the Jacksons (傑克森家族)

例 They love the Smiths.
他們愛史密斯家族的人。

有些地名或國名前面要加the

例 the Arctic
北極

例 the Nile
尼羅河

例 the Rocky Mountains
洛基山脈

例 the Netherlands
荷蘭。

例 the Philippines
菲律賓

例 the United States
美國

例 the Republic of Ireland
愛爾蘭共和國（共和國Republic或王國Kingdom前面要加the）

請在(a) (b) (c) (d) 中選出正確答案（可能是複選）

1. He gave me ____.

   (a) a pencil (b) an pencil (c) a iPad (d) an iPad

2. I have ____.

   (a) a question (b) 2 questions (c) a questions (d) 2 question

3. I need ____.

   (a) a friend (b) friends (c) a friends (d) friend

4. He is ____ father of Jessica.

   (a) a (b) the (c) this(d) that

5. She has a dog. ____ dog is white.

   (a) A (b) The (c) Her (d) An

6. I met ____ President of the United States.

   (a) a (b) the (c) this (d) that

7. The Duncans ____ in Africa.

   (a) live (b) lives (c) lived (d) living

8. 何者正確？

   (a) Cats are animals. (b) A cat is an animal.

   (c) Cat is animal. (d) Cat are animal.

9. Fiona is ____ girl.

   (a) a smart (b) an nice (c) a American (d) an American

10. Kathy has ____.

   (a) a money (b) a dollar (c) dollar (d) money

1. (a) (d) 名詞第一個字母是子音，前面用a。第一個字母是母音，前面用an。
2. (a) (b) 單數名詞前面加a，複數名詞前面不加a。
3. (a) (b) 單數名詞前面一定加a，所以 (d) 是錯的。
4. (b) Jessica的父親應只有一位，所以前面用定冠詞。
5. (b) (c) 這裡指她的狗，所以用定冠詞或代名詞所有格。
6. (b) 美國只有一位總統，所以用定冠詞。
7. (a) (c) Duncan一家人爲複數。
8. (a) (b) 單數名詞前面一定加a。
9. (a) (d) 形容詞第一個字母是子音，前面用a。第一個字母是母音，前面用an。
10. (b) (d) dollar爲可數，單數可數名詞前面一定加a。money爲不可數，前面不加a。

Part · 4

名詞

名詞就是指人、事、物、地。

人：man (男人)，woman (女人)，teacher (老師)，John (約翰)

事：music (音樂)，love (愛)，information (資訊)，hint (暗示)

物：table (桌子)，kiwi (奇異果)，money (錢)，monkey (猴子)

地：home (家)，office (辦公室)，town (鎮)，Russia (俄羅斯)

名詞可分成可數或不可數。前者如人、狗、樹等。後者如空氣、水、陽光等。

你可以說一隻狗、兩個桌子，所以是可數。但你能說一個空氣或一個水嗎? 所以空氣和水是不可數。

英文中有單數、複數的差別，單數就是正好一個、複數是超過一個。
可數名詞可分為單數、複數。大部分情況下，單數可數名詞字尾加上s就變成複數。

單數	複數
a bag (一個袋子)	**two bags (兩個袋子)**
a dog (一隻狗)	**three dogs (三隻狗)**
a car (一輛車)	**ten cars (十輛車)**

名詞字尾若是 **s, x, z, ch, sh**時，複數加**es**。		
單數	複數	中文
bus	**buses**	公車
box	**boxes**	盒子
match	**matches**	火柴
church	**churches**	教堂
waltz	**waltzes**	華爾滋
quiz	**quizzes**（多一個**z**）	測驗

下列名詞複數要加**es**		
單數	複數	中文
hero	**heroes**	英雄
echo	**echoes**	回音
potato	**potatoes**	馬鈴薯
tomato	**tomatoes**	番茄

名詞字尾是**y**，且字尾前一字母是子音時，複數改為去掉**y**加**ies**。		
單數	複數	中文
baby	**babies**	嬰兒
party	**parties**	派對
penny	**pennies**	分
country	**countries**	國家
lady	**ladies**	女士
city	**cities**	城市

大部分情形下字尾是 **is,** 複數去掉 **is** 加上**es**。		
單數	複數	中文
crisis	**crises**	危機
basis	**bases**	基礎
oasis	**oases**	綠洲

下列名詞字尾是 **f** 或 **fe**， 複數通常將 **f** 改成 **v** ，字尾變成 **ves**。		
單數	複數	中文
loaf	**loaves**	條
knife	**knives**	刀
life	**lives**	生命
wife	**wives**	妻子

名詞改複數的不規則變化		
單數	複數	中文
man	**men**	男人
woman	**women**	女人
child	**children**	小孩
person	**people**	人
tooth	**teeth**	牙齒
foot	**feet**	腳
mouse	**mice**	老鼠
goose	**geese**	鵝
datum	**data**	資料

下列表格中的字單複數相同		
單數	複數	中文
sheep	**sheep**	綿羊
fish	**fish**	魚
deer	**deer**	鹿
aircraft	**aircraft**	飛機

下列名詞只有複數沒有單數		
glasses	眼鏡	眼鏡有兩片玻璃，所以用複數。
trousers	褲子	褲子有兩條褲管，所以用複數。
jeans	牛仔褲	牛仔褲有兩條褲管，所以用複數。
scissors	剪刀	剪刀有兩個刀片

例 My trousers are very long.
我的褲子很長。(用複數be動詞are)

例 My scissors are on my desk.
我的剪刀在我的書桌上。(用複數be動詞are)

英文還有複合名詞，也就是一個名詞是由一個以上的字所組成。複合名詞改成複數時，將主要的名詞加上s。

單數	複數	中文
son-in-law	**sons-in-law**	女婿 (法律上的兒子)
passer-by	**passers-by**	過路行人

不可數名詞都用單數。

例 Milk is delicious! (牛奶不可數，所以用is。)
牛奶好喝！

例 Water is transparent.
水是透明的。

例 Health and education are very important.
健康和教育很重要。(健康和教育兩個不可數名詞合在一起就變複數，所以用are。)

不可數名詞如果加上單位就可以數了，用法為：數量+單位 + of + 不可數名詞。

例如兩杯水…two cups of water。因爲是兩杯，所以cup加s。

a pair of spectacles...一副眼鏡
2 bags of rice...兩袋米 (bag加s)
3 bars of chocolate...三條巧克力 (bar加s)
2 jars of honey...兩罐蜂蜜 (jar加s)

有些名詞有一種以上的意思，其中一種可數，另一種不可以數。

紙不可數，所以不能說a paper。兩張紙要說 2 pieces of paper。如果paper當成論文就可數，例如：two papers...兩篇論文。

Light (光)不可數，但如果light當成燈泡就可數，2 lights...兩個燈泡。

有時不可數名詞看起來變成可數，是因為將單位省略。

例 Please give us 2 coffees.
請給我們兩杯咖啡。(省略了cups of)

例 I bought three waters.
我買了三瓶礦泉水。(省略了bottles of)

有些名詞字尾有s，看起來像複數，實際上是單數。

例 Economics is a very difficult subject.
經濟學是一個門非常困難的學科。

例 This news is very important.
這個新聞非常重要。

所謂集合名詞是指一群人、事、物，可用單數或複數。當我們認為這名詞代表整個群體時就用單數，但如果是其中一些個人時就用複數。

例 His family live in different areas.
他的家人住在不同的地區。

例 His family is very unpopular.
他的家人非常不受歡迎。(這裡的家人指整體，所以用單數。)

常見的集合名詞還有government (政府)，army (軍隊)，committee (委員會)等。

下列名詞第一個字母要大寫。

1. 人名第一個字母要大寫。

   George Washington (喬治華盛頓), Bill Gates (比爾蓋茲), Ming Tong Lee (李明同).

2. 學校、公司、組織名第一個字母要大寫。

   Harvard University (哈佛大學), the United Nations (聯合國), Rolls Royce (勞斯萊斯).

3. 地名第一個字母要大寫

   Taiwan (台灣), Paris (巴黎), the Red Sea (紅海), Chien Kuo Road (建國路).

4. 月份、星期幾、節日第一個字母要大寫

   May (五月), Monday (星期一), Easter (復活節).

5. 電影、書籍、藝術作品名稱第一個字母要大寫

Alice in Wonderland (愛麗絲夢遊仙境), The Matrix (駭客任務)

6. 稱呼第一個字母要大寫

Ms. (小姐), Mrs. (夫人), Mr. (先生), Dr. (醫師), President Lincoln (林肯總統)

有些名詞沒有性別區分	
baby	小寶貝 (不分男女)
child	男孩或女孩
infant	男嬰或女嬰
parent	父或母
cousin	表哥或表姊

有些名詞有性別區分			
actor	男演員	**actress**	女演員
bride	新娘	**bridegroom**	新郎
hero	英雄	**heroine**	女英雄
host	男主人	**hostess**	女主人
prince	王子	**princess**	公主
waiter	男侍	**waitress**	女侍

名詞的所有格...名詞後面加's

Jenny's coat (珍妮的外套), John's father (約翰的爸爸), Nancy's goat (南西的山羊)

若名詞是複數，字尾本身就是s，所有格就直接將'放在字尾

A boys' school (男校), Students' idea (學生的點子), the girls' room (女孩的房間)

若名詞字尾就是s，所有格就直接將'放在字尾

Thomas' iPad (湯瑪斯的iPad)

複合名詞的所有格，將's加在最後一個字

My daughter-in-law's coach (我媳婦的教練)

回答時名詞可省略

例 Is that John's bike?
那是約翰的腳踏車嗎？

例 No, it's Mary's.
不，是瑪莉的。(省略bike)

名詞的所有格也可用介係詞of來表示

John's plane = the plane of John約翰的飛機

The girls' room = the room of the girls女孩的房間

The sailors' boat = the boat of the sailors水手的船

常見的名詞簡寫

ad = advertisement廣告

doc = doctor醫生

exam = examination考試

gas = gasoline汽油

gym = gymnasium體育館

fridge = refrigerator冰箱

常見的組合字

brunch = breakfast + lunch早午餐

motel = motor car + hotel汽車旅館

spork = spoon + fork湯匙叉子合在一起的餐具

有些動詞 + er或or 變名詞

work (工作)→ worker (工人)

make (製造)→maker (製造者)

peel (削)→peeler (削水果刀)

act (表演)→actor (演員)

練習題

請在 (a) (b) (c) (d) 中選出正確答案（可能是複選）

1. Health ____ important!

   (a) is (b) am (c) are (d) were

2. ____ is the President now.

   (a) Donald trump (b) donald trump (c) donald Trump (d) Donald Trump

3. ____ is black and white.

   (a) Johns bike (b) John's bike (c) The bike of John's (d) The bike of John

4. A: Is that your book?

   B: No, it's ____.

   (a) Jim's (b) Jim (c) he (d) his

5. Princess ____ is 25 years old.

   (a) Diana (b) Mary (c) Mike (d) John

6. I bought ____.

   (a) 2 waters (b) 2 bottles of water (c) 2 water (d) water

7. I have ____.

   (a) 3 jars of honey (b) 2 bars of rice (c) 3 pieces of paper (d) 5 loaves of milk

8. It has ____.

   (a) 2 foot (b) 2 feet (c) 20 tooth (d) 20 teeth

9. ____ are Canadians.

(a) One lady and three gentleman (b) Two ladys and three gentlemen (c) Two ladies lady and two gentlemen (d) One lady and three gentleman

10. Please give me ____!

(a) a love (b) love (c) an love (d) loves

1. (a) health 是不可數名詞，要用is。
2. (d) 人名第一個字母要大寫。
3. (b) (d) 人名所有格的正確表示法。
4. (a) (d) (d) 是所有格代名詞。
5. (a) (b) princess是公主，後面要接女生名字。
6. (a) (b) (d) (a) 是 (b) 的縮寫，表示兩瓶水。水是不可數名詞，所以 (c) 是錯的， (d) 是對的。
7. (a) (c) bar是條，不是米的單位。Loaves是吐司，而非牛奶的單位。
8. (b) (d) foot和tooth是單數，feet和teeth是複數。
9. (c) lady的複數是ladies，gentleman的複數是gentle men，如同man的複數是men。
10. (b) love是不可數名詞，沒有複數，前面也不加冠詞。

Part 5

介系詞

介系詞後面可能接名詞或代名詞受格，不會接代名詞主格。

例 Don is looking for Todd. (for是介系詞，Todd名詞)
唐正在尋找陶德。

例 Don is looking for him. (him是代名詞受格)
唐正在尋找他。

be動詞+looking for是一個片語，表示：尋找。

例 Mary talks to they. (╳) (to是介系詞，they是主格，要改成them)
瑪莉和他們說話。

介系詞後面可能接動名詞 (V + ing)，但永遠不會接原型動詞。
所謂動名詞 (V + ing)也就是將動詞後面加上ing，詞性等於名詞，以後章節會提到。

例 I ate my lunch before coming. (✓)
I ate my lunch before come. (╳)
我來之前已吃過午飯。

常用介系詞

1. above...在…上面

例 USA is above Mexico.
美國位於墨西哥上方。

例 The helicopter hovered above the farm.
直升機在農場上方徘徊。

2. about...關於

例 He knows everything about me.
他知道關於我的每件事。

例 The lawyer did nothing about it.
關於這件事律師什麼也沒做。

3. according to...依據

例 According to this book, he finally succeeded.
根據這本書，他終於成功了。

4. across...橫跨

例 She swam across the river.
她游過河。

5. after...在⋯後面

例 She closed the door after her.
她關上了身後的門。

例 March comes after February.
三月在二月之後。

6. along ...沿著

例 We rowed along the shore
我們沿著岸邊划船。

7. among...在…之中

例 I found my hat among the luggage.
我在行李中發現我的帽子。

例 Jane is popular among her classmates.
珍在同學中受歡迎。

8. around...環繞

例 Look at the trees around the playground!
看看遊樂場周圍的樹！

around也可指接近某時間

例 Ted woke up around 6:30.
泰德接近六點半起床。

9. as...當作介系詞時可表示某種身分

I worked as the supervisor.

我的工作是管理者。

He was nominated as a Secretary of State.

他被提名為國務卿。

as也可指：當作

例 He used the umbrella as a weapon.
他用雨傘作為武器。

例 You shouldn't treat those people as garbage.
你不應該把那些人當成垃圾。

10. at...位於某一地點

例 He is waiting at the entrance.
他正在入口處等候。

例 I live at 123 Hobart Street.
我住在霍巴特街123號。

例 She got off at the next station.
她在下一站下車。

at可指在某一時間

at noon--在中午，at dinnertime--在晚餐時間，

at lunchtime--在午餐時間，

at bedtime--在睡覺時間，at midnight--在午夜，

at night--晚上。

例 I have a meeting at 9am.
我上午九點有一個會議。(整點用at)

例 Tina stayed with her boyfriend at Christmas.
蒂娜聖誕節和她的男朋友在一起。(節日用at)

at可指在幾歲

例 I started my business at 51.
我51歲開始我的事業。

例 The hero died at 89.
英雄89歲去世。

11. behind...在…後面

例 Hina put her hands behind her back.
喜娜將雙手放在背後。

例 The park is behind the fire station.
公園在消防局後面。

12. below...在…下面

例 A river runs below the bridge.
橋下有一條河流過。

13. between...介於…與…之間

例 Thomas sat between Ronald and me.
湯瑪斯坐在隆納和我之間。

例 He will be here between 7am and 8am.
他上午7點到8點之間會來這裡。

14. by...在某時間以前

例 They will get married by the end of July.
他們七月底前結婚。

例 Come back by five o'clock!
五點前回來！

by的另一用法為藉由某種交通工具

例 Jack will go there by bus, not by train.
傑克會坐公車而非火車去那裏。

by還可表示被某人完成

例 I've read some books by Ernest Hemingway.
我讀過一些海明威的書。

例 The lion was killed by the hunter.
獅子被獵人所殺。

例 This is the best painting by Van Gogh.
這是梵谷最棒的畫。

by可表示靠近

例 I sat by my partner.
我坐靠近我的夥伴。

例 The cafe is beside the hotel.
餐廳靠近飯店。(beside = 靠近)

15. during...在某期間

例 He lived next to me during the summer vacation.
暑假期間他住我隔壁。

16. for...為了…

例 I did it for you.
我是為你做的。

例 We stopped for a chat.
我們停下來為了聊天。

例 The knife is for opening envelopes.
這把刀用來開信封。

for 可表示時間或距離

例 I waited for a very long time.
我等了很長的時間。

例 She has studied Physics for five years.
她已經學習了五年物理學。

17. From...從

例 I'm from Malaysia.
我從馬來西亞來的。

例 The closet is made from pine.
衣櫃由松樹製成。

from…to… (從…到…)

例 That store is open from dawn to dusk.
那商店從早開到晚。

例 I travelled from Asia to Europe.
我從亞洲旅行到歐洲。

18. in...在…裡面

例 Her toy is in the car.
她的玩具在車裡。

例 Look at the girl in the picture.
看看照片中的女孩。

例 I have a lot of money in my pocket.
我的口袋裡有很多錢。

→表示地點時 in 是指範圍比較大的區域，而 at 是指範圍比較小且位置較精確的地點。

例 I lived in Pittsburgh Pennsylvania.
我住在賓夕法尼亞州匹茲堡市。

例 This is the best novel in the world.
這是世界上最好的小說。

→in 指某月、某季節、某年、某世紀或較長的時間，前面提到 at 是用在較短的時間，例如：at noon 在中午。

例 I met my wife in 2017.
我在2017年遇到了我的妻子。

例 In summer we like to go to the beach.
夏天我們喜歡去海灘。

例 The seminar was held in November.
研討會於11月舉行。

例 Hopefully we can move to Mars in the next century.
希望我們可以在下個世紀搬到火星。

例 We will be back in a few days.
我們將在幾天內回來。

例 I always read the newspaper in the morning, take a nap in the afternoon, then go home in the evening.
我向來早上讀報紙，下午睡個午覺，傍晚回家。

→in 可表示穿甚麼衣服

例 Brenda is the girl in the purple dress.
布蘭達是穿紫色衣服的女孩。

例 You really look good in a suit.
你穿西裝真的很好看。

19. in front of...在…前面

例 She smiled at the man in front of her.
她對著她面前的男人微笑。

例 Please don't stand in front of the camera.
請不要站在相機前面。

20. into...進入…之中

例 Get into the car! It's raining!
進來車子裡！外面在下雨！

例 Emily ran into the living room.
艾米麗跑進客廳。

→run into 或 bump into 是片語，表示巧遇某人。（上例中run into是跑進某個地方，所以要看前後文決定片語的意義。）

例 I ran into my old friend last night.
昨晚我遇到了我的老朋友

例 Jason bumped into his boss on the street.
傑森在街上碰到他的老闆。

21. like...像…

例 Don't work like a dog.
不要工作得像條狗。

例 Paul looks like his father.
保羅看起來像他的父親。

22. of...屬於…的

例 He is the President of Taiwan.
他是台灣的總統。

例 This house is the property of the church.
這房子是教會的財產。

23. on...在…表面

例 I love the painting on the wall.
我喜歡牆上的畫。

例 Put your money on the table.
把你的錢放在桌子上

例 My puppy is lying on the carpet.
我的小狗正躺在地毯上。

例 We found some information on this page.
我們在這頁上面找到了一些資訊。

例 I won't forget the smile on his face.
我不會忘記他臉上的笑容。

On...可表示交通方式

We went to the supermarket on foot.

我們徒步走到超級市場。

I saw some familiar faces on the plane.

我在飛機上看到一些熟悉的面孔。

On...用在表示特定日子

例 I have to call him on Monday morning.
我星期一早上必須打電話給他。

例 Uncle Eddie's birthday is on 15 November.
艾迪叔叔的生日是11月15日。

例 Let's have a party on New Year's Day.
讓我們在元旦舉行派對。

24. out of...脫離

例 She ran out of the building.
她跑出了大樓。

例 My friend, take it out of the box.
我的朋友，把它從箱子拿出來。

25. over...超過、在…之上

例 That lady is over 35 but she looks so young.
那位女士超過35歲，但她看起來很年輕。

例 This yacht is over 50 million.
這艘遊艇超過5000萬。

26. under...還不到、在…之下

例 My teacher is under 40.
我老師不到40歲。

例 The temperature outside is under 0 degrees Celsius.
外面的溫度在攝氏0度以下。

例 We enjoy sheltering under a tree.
我們享受在樹下遮陰。

27. up...上

例 Do the prices of cars go up?
汽車價格上漲嗎？

例 They both went up the stairs.
他們倆個都走上樓。

例 Salmon can swim up the streams.
鮭魚可以游泳溯溪而上。

28. till...直到

例 He didn't email me till today.
他直到今天才寫email給我。

29. past...超過

例 It's 10 past 6 now.
現在是6點10分。

例 Walk past the bank then you will see the post office.
走過銀行，你會看到郵局。

30. since...自從

例 Ian is allergic to milk since birth.
伊恩從出生後就對牛奶過敏。

31. through...穿越

例 They walked through the woods.
他們走過樹林。

例 The train went through the tunnel.
火車穿過隧道。

32. to...朝…方向

例 I moved to Spain in 2016.
我在2016年搬到了西班牙。

例 They drove to Nevada.
他們開車去內華達。

例 It's twenty to eight.
現在差20分到8點。

例 It's only three weeks to Thanksgiving.
離感恩節只有三個禮拜。

例 I look forward to seeing you.
我期待著與你見面。

注意：to是介係詞，所以後面接動名詞 (see + ing)。

33. toward...朝向某個時間或地點

例 She brought it to me toward midnight.
將近午夜時她把它帶給我。

例 Peggy finally stood up and walked toward him.
佩姬終於站起來走向他。

... toward可表示對某人某事的感覺

例 I don't know the government's attitude toward this bill.
我不知道政府對這個法案的態度。

34. with...陪伴，與…同在

例 Don't worry! He will go with you.
別擔心！他會和你一起去的。

例 I live with my wife and kids.
我和我的妻子還有小孩一起生活。

例 Never fight with your brother!
永遠不要和你的兄弟打架！

with可表示同意

例 Are you with me or against me?
你同意我或反對我？

with...使用

例 Larry killed his enemy with a knife.
賴瑞用刀殺了他的敵人。

with...有…

例 The man with a red moustache is Andrew.
有紅鬍子的人是安德魯。

例 We bought a new television with a large screen.
我們買了一個大螢幕的新電視。

例 The dog with the pink collar is mine.
戴著粉紅色狗鍊的狗是我的。

注意：上面是後位修飾法，也就是用**with**後面的名詞形容前面的名詞。例如：紅鬍子形容安德魯，大螢幕形容電視，粉紅色狗鍊形容狗。

請在(a) (b) (c) (d) 中選出正確答案（可能是複選）

1. Talk ____ me, please!

   (a) for (b) at (c) to (d) up

2. After ____, he took a shower.

   (a) run (b) ran (c) running (d) is running

3. Johnson arrived in ____.

   (a) night (b) the morning (c) dinnertime (d) October

4. I saw a girl ____ purple hair.

   (a) for (b) on (c) in (d) with

5. I look forward ____ seeing you.

   (a) for (b) on (c) to (d) with

6. His wedding day is ____ 8/25.

   (a) in (b) on (c) for (d) at

7. I remember the look ____ his face.

   (a) in (b) on (c) for (d) at

8. Larry eats ____ a hungry wolf.

   (a) across (b) toward (c) like (d) as

9. He is a hero according ____ your word.

   (a) to (b) on (c) for (d) at

10. Ron worked ____ dusk to dawn.

    (a) from (b) between (c) with (d) below

1. (c) 對某人說話的片語是talk to。
2. (c) 介係詞after後面要用V+ing。
3. (b) (d) night和dinnertime前面用at。
4. (d) 有著紫色頭髮的女孩，with放在名詞後面作為後位修飾，表示：有著。
5. (c) look forward to是片語，表示：期待。後面接V+ing。
6. (b) 日期前面用on。
7. (b) 在…上面用on，look on his face意思是：他臉上的表情。
8. (c) like可表示：像。Eat like a hungry wolf: 吃得像飢餓的狼。
9. (a) according to是片語：依據。
10. (a) 從…到…的片語是：from... to...。

Part 6

代名詞

代名詞變化表		
主格	所有格	受格
I	**my**	**me**
you	**your**	**you**
he	**his**	**him**
she	**her**	**her**
it	**its**	**it**
we	**our**	**us**
they	**their**	**them**

到目前為止我們已經討論過代名詞的主格、所有格、受格。現在重新複習一遍。

例 I gave my book to her.
我給我的書給她。

上面例子中，I是主格放在句首，my是所有格放在名詞前面，her是受格，放在動詞或介係詞的後面。

例 Did you drive him to your home?
你開車載他去你家嗎？

上面例子中，you是主格，your是所有格，him是受格。

注意： Its和It's的不同。Its是所有格，表示：它的。

It's = It is，It's 9am....現在上午9點。

It's 也可等於It has。

例 My house is big. It's got five bedrooms. (It has got five bedrooms.)
我的房子很大。有五間臥室。

顧名思義，代名詞就是用來代替名詞。若少了代名詞句子可能會一直重複相同的字。

例 I love my cat. My cat is black.
我喜歡我的貓，我的貓是黑色的。

可以改成:

I love my cat. It is black.

例 John is my classmate. John is very tall.
約翰是我的朋友。約翰很高。

John is my classmate. He is very tall.
約翰是我的朋友。他很高。

練習題：將畫線名詞改成代名詞

1. Joseph likes Sabrina.
2. That is Diane's umbrella.
3. Mary and I went home.
4. I know you and your family.
5. My PC doesn't work.

解答：

1. He likes her.
2. That is her umbrella.
3. We went home.
4. I know you.
5. It doesn't work.

不定代名詞用來指不特定的人事物。

Everyone (每個人，也可用 **everybody**), **everything**（每件事）都用單數動詞。

例 Everybody likes ice cream.
每個人都喜歡冰淇淋。

例 Everything is fine.
每件事都好。

例 Everyone has a dream.
每個人都有一個夢想。

someone (有些人，也可用 **somebody**), **something** (有些事) 都用單數動詞。

例 Someone is dancing in the park.
有人在公園裡跳舞。

例 Something happens.
有事情發生。

例 That is somebody's brother. (somebody用所有格，後面加's)
那是某人的兄弟。

anyone (任何人，也可用 **anybody**), **anything** (任何事) 都用單數動詞。

例 Is it anybody's pet?
這是任何人的寵物嗎？

例 Does anybody know?
有人知道嗎

例 The blind man cannot see anything.
盲人看不到任何東西。

no one (沒有人，也可用 **nobody**), **nothing** (沒有事情) 都用單數動詞。

例 Nobody is perfect!
沒有人是完美的！

例 It's no one's fault.
誰都沒錯。

例 Nothing is too difficult.
沒有什麼太難。

注意：**not any = no, not anything = nothing, not anybody = nobody.**

The blind man cannot see anything. = The blind man can see nothing.

I don't hate anybody. = I hate nobody.

some: 有些人， **others:** 其他人。

例 Some think he is a good musician. Others think he is not good.
有些人認為他是一個很好的音樂家。其他人認為他不好。

one **(**單數**)**、 **ones** **(**複數**)**可避免不必要的重複。

例 I have two nieces. Molly is the tall one and Elaine is the short one.
我有兩個侄女。莫莉是高的那個，伊萊恩是矮的那個。(one取代niece)

例 My pens are stolen. I need some new ones.
我的筆被偷。我需要一些新的。(ones取代pens，注意：ones用複數，表示：一些筆。)

one: 其中一個，**the other:**剩下的那個。

例 I had two scarfs. One was red and the other was purple.
我有兩條圍巾。一條是紅的，另一條是紫的。

one: 其中一個，**another:**另一個。

例 He has one job in the day and another at night.
他白天有一份工作，晚上有另一份工作。（他可能總共三分工作，所有用another，不用the other。）

Each: 每個人

例 Each has his own thoughts.
每個人都有自己的想法。

Few 可當成很少人

例 Few know about his story.
很少人知道他的故事。

Many 可當成很多人

例 Many came to the ceremony.
許多人來參加典禮。

several： 兩個人以上但不太多，**more:**更多人

例 Several left the meeting, but more attended.
幾個人離開了會議，但更多的人出席了會議。

most: 大多數人

例 Most disagreed with his crazy idea.
大多數人不同意他的瘋狂想法。

else: 其他的

例 Do you want anything else?
你需要其它的任何東西嗎？

例 You can ask somebody else.
你可以問別人。

例 No one else can help him.
沒有別人可以幫助他。

each other: 兩者互相

例 Tom and Sandy love each other.
湯姆和山蒂彼此相愛。

例 We sent each other flowers.
我們互相送花。

例 They like each other's poems.
他們喜歡彼此的詩歌。(each other用所有格，後面加's)

one another: 三者 (或以上)互相

例 Those six roommates should help one another.
那六個室友應該互相幫助。

例 We often share one another's jokes. (one another用所有格，後面加's)
我們經常分享彼此的笑話。

both: 兩者皆是，**either:** 兩者中的一個，**neither:** 兩者皆非。**both** 為複數，**either** 和 **neither** 用單數。

例 Coffee or tea? I think both are good.
咖啡還是茶？我覺得兩者都好。

例 Coffee or tea? I think neither is good.
咖啡還是茶？我覺得兩者都不好。

例 I have cake and muffin. You can have either.
我有蛋糕和馬芬。你可以挑其中一個。

例 I have cake and muffin. You can have both.
我有蛋糕和馬芬。你兩個都可以吃。

both, each, some, most, many, one, none 後面可加 **of** 再加名詞或代名詞。

例 Both of them love music.
他們兩個都喜歡音樂。(用複數動詞)

例 Each of the doctors has an office.
每個醫生都有自己的辦公室。(用單數動詞)

例 Some of us want to visit the zoo.
我們當中有些人想去動物園。(用複數動詞)

例 Most of us never did that before.
我們當中大多數人從來沒有這樣做過。(用複數動詞)

例 Many of us live here.
我們當中許多人住在這裡。(用複數動詞)

例 One of us is a soldier.
我們當中的一個是士兵。(用單數動詞)

例 None of us hates that movie.
我們當中沒人討厭那部電影。(用單數動詞)

所有格代名詞

所有格代名詞	中文
mine	我的
yours	你的
his	他的
hers	她的
its	它的
ours	我們的
yours	你們的
theirs	他們的

所有格代名詞...可用來代替：所有格 ＋ 名詞

例 You Love your car, I love mine.
你愛你的車，我愛我的。(mine 代替my car)

例 My books are new. Hers are old.
我的書是新的，她的書是舊的。(Hers代替her books)

A Is that your classroom?

那是你們的教室嗎？

B No, it's theirs.

不，是他們的。(theirs代替their classroom)

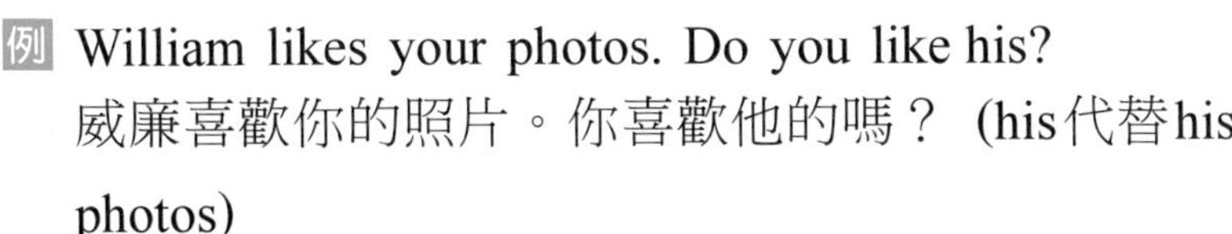

例 William likes your photos. Do you like his?
威廉喜歡你的照片。你喜歡他的嗎？ (his代替his photos)

例 This is my cell phone. That's her cell phone. (✓)
這是我的手機。那是她的手機。

例 This cell phone is mine. That cell phone is hers. (✓)
這手機是我的。那手機是她的。

例 Sam drinks his coffee. I drink mine. (✓)
Sam drinks his coffee. I drink my coffee. (✓)
Sam drinks his coffee. I drink mine coffee. (╳)
山姆喝他的咖啡。我喝我的。

例 I like your plan, but mine is better.
我喜歡你的計劃，但我的更好。

例 Your hat is red. Hers is blue.
你的帽子是紅色的。她的是藍色

例 My ticket costs 100 bucks, yours?
我的門票100塊錢。你的呢？

反射代名詞

反射代名詞如同鏡子般反射主格	
反射代名詞	中文
myself	我自己
yourself	你自己
himself	他自己
herself	她自己
itself	它自己
ourselves	我們自己
yourselves	你們自己
themselves	他們自己

例 I saw myself in the mirror. (✓)
I saw me in the mirror. (✕)
我在鏡子裡看到自己。

例 You should love yourself. (✓)
You should love you. (✕)
你應該愛你自己。

比較下面兩句的不同

例 John sent himself a copy.
約翰送了一份拷貝給自己。

例 John sent him a copy.
約翰送了一份拷貝給他。(這裡的他是指別人，而非約翰自己)

例 My dog hurt itself.
我的狗弄傷了自己。

例 My dog hurt it.
我的狗弄傷了它。(這裡的它並非狗自己)

by ＋ 反射代名詞...表示單獨完成

例 They finished this project by themselves.
他們靠自己完成了這個計畫。

例 I cooked this dish by myself.
我自己完成了這道菜。

反射代名詞放在名詞或代名詞後面，用來強調。

例 I myself made these cookies.
我自己做了這些餅乾。(強調自己做的，如果將myself去掉，整句意思不受影響。)

例 The test itself isn't difficult, but we need more time.
測試本身並不困難，但是我們需要更多的時間。(強調測試本身，如果將itself去掉，整句話意思仍然一樣。)

例 I met the President himself.
我遇到了總統本人。(強調是總統本人，如果將himself去掉，整句話意思仍然一樣。)

虛擬主詞

It...表示時間、日期、天氣、距離。

例 It's nearly one o'clock.
差不多一點了。(it指時間)

例 It's my birthday.
今天是我的生日。(it指日期)

例 It's raining.
正在下雨。(it指天氣)

例 It's 100 kilometers from here to Taichung.
這裡到台中距離100公里。(it指距離)

例 It's very comfortable in my new apartment.
我的新公寓環境很舒服。(it指環境)

例 It's very cold outside.
外面很冷。（it指天氣）

例 It's 2017. Everybody uses cell phones.
現在是2017。每個人都使用手機。（it指時間）

虛擬主詞 there + be 動詞

例 There are some students in the classroom.
教室裡有一些學生。

英文中不會說：The classroom has some students. 因為學生可能會在教室裡面上課，但學生並非屬於教室。

例 I have a meeting this evening.
我今天傍晚有個會議。

例 There's a meeting this evening.
今天傍晚有個會議。(並沒有強調是誰的會議)

例 There were lots of cats in the playground yesterday. (✓)
Playground had lots of cats yesterday. (✕)
昨天在遊樂場上有很多貓。(貓並非屬於遊樂場)

例 Is there any orange juice in the fridge?
冰箱裡有橙汁嗎？

Yes, there is some.
是的，有一些。

No, there isn't any.
不，沒有任何橙汁。

請在(a) (b) (c) (d) 中選出正確答案（可能是複選）

1. ____ some tigers in this zoo.

   (a) There is (b) There are (c) There was (d) There were

2. Fanny did her homework. I did ____.

   (a) my (b) my homework (c) mine (d) mine homework

3. ____ like Jazz.

   (a) Some of we (b) Some of us (c) We some (d) Some us

4. ____ of them loves that movie.

   (a) None (b) Many (c) Both (d) Most

5. Eric and Ivy like ____.

   (a) one another (b) each other (c) each another

   (d) oneother

6. Tuna or salmon? ____ is yummy.

   (a) Both (b) All (c) Either (d) Neither

7. ____ are doctors.

   (a) Several (b) Few (c) Little (d) Everybody

8. I have 2 cars. One is white. ____ is red.

   (a) The other (b) another (c) each other (d) one another

9. There are some desks. The green ____ are hers.

   (a) one (b) ones (c) desks (d) something

10. ____ happened.

    (a) Someone (b) No one (c) Something (d) Nothing

1. (b) (d) some tigers是複數，所以要用There are或There were。
2. (b) (c) 在這裡mine = my homework。用mine可避免重複。
3. (b) of後面一定接受格，沒有We some這種說法。
4. (a) loves表示前面一定是第三人稱單數，只有none符合，其他 (b) (c) (d) 都用複數。
5. (b) 兩個人互相，所以用each other。
6. (c) (d) either或neither後面都可接單數動詞is。
7. (a) (b) little用在不可數，Everybody後面一定接單數。
8. (a) 兩個中的另一個用the other。
9. (b) (c) desks可用ones取代避免重複。
10. (c) (d) 事情才會發生，人不會發生，故(a) (b) 是錯的。

Part 7

形容詞

從下列句子中可看出形容詞的位置用法幾乎和中文相同...放在名詞前面，或者放在動詞後面。

例 Tommy has 2 cute dogs.
湯米有2隻可愛的狗。

例 Cindy has a black car.
辛迪有一輛黑色的車。

例 I like white coffee.
我喜歡白咖啡

例 This is an old song.
這是一首老歌。

例 Peter's shirt is blue.
彼得的襯衫是藍色的。

例 The table is wooden.
桌子是木製的。

例 The girl is happy.
這個女孩很開心。

例 The coffee keeps me awake.
咖啡使我保持清醒。

例 He makes me glad.
他讓我快樂。

但如果遇到something, anything, everyone, anyone這類的字，形容詞要放在後面。

例 I have something important to say. (✓)
I have important something to say. (✕)
我有一件重要的事想要說。

例 Is there anything wrong?
有任何事不對嗎

例 I know someone nice in this office. (✓)
I know a nice someone in this office. (✕) (形容詞要放在someone後面，something, anything, everyone, anyone這類的字前面不加冠詞a或定冠詞the。)
我知道這個辦公室裡有一個人很好。

形容詞的原級、比較級、最高級
通常單音節的形容詞在字尾加上 er, est 構成比較級、最高級...所謂規則變化。

例如：tall (原級), taller (比較級), tallest (最高級)

例 Jack is tall, William is taller, but Nathan is the tallest.
傑克很高，威廉更高，但納森最高。(形容詞最高級前面要加the)

常見的單音節形容詞規則變化			
原級	比較級	最高級	中文
high	**higher**	**highest**	高
fast	**faster**	**fastest**	快
large	**larger**	**largest**	大
nice	**nicer**	**nicest**	好
cheap	**cheaper**	**cheapest**	便宜
strong	**stronger**	**strongest**	強壯
有些單音節形容詞規則變化要重複字尾			
thin	**thinner**	**thinnest**	薄
sad	**sadder**	**saddest**	悲傷
hot	**hotter**	**hottest**	熱
big	**bigger**	**biggest**	大

例 Alex ran very fast, but Ron ran faster.
亞歷克斯跑得很快，但羅恩跑得更快。

例 I need a bigger burger.
我需要一個更大的漢堡

例 LA is the largest city in California.
洛杉磯是加州最大的城市。(形容詞最高級前面要加the)

大多數兩音節以上形容詞，比較級前面加more (較多) 或 less (較少), 最高級前面加most (最)或least (最不)。

例 Helen is beautiful, Karen is more beautiful. But Karen is not the most beautiful girl in school.
海倫是美麗的，凱倫更美麗。但凱倫不是學校最美麗的女孩。

例 This room is comfortable, that room is less comfortable.
這間房間很舒適，那間房間比較不舒適。

例 That's the least funny joke!
那是最不好笑的笑話！

下列形容詞是例外，雖是兩音節，卻可不用 more, most, less, least等，而可加er表示比較級，加est表示最高級。

原級	比較級	最高級	中文
happy	**happier** 去**y**加**ier**	**happiest** 去**y**加**iest**	快樂
easy	**easier** 去**y**加**ier**	**easiest.** 去**y**加**iest**	容易
busy	**busier** 去**y**加**ier**	**busiest** 去**y**加**iest**	忙
simple	**simpler**	**simplest**	簡單

例 She looks happier now.
她現在看起來更開心了。

例 This is the simplest question.
這是最簡單的問題。

例 Aron becomes busier.
阿倫變得更忙。

不規則變化			
原級	比較級	最高級	中文
bad	**worse**	**worst**	壞
good	**better**	**best**	好
many	**more**	**most**	多 (可數)
much	**more**	**most**	多 (不可數)
late	**later**	**latest**	時間上的先後
late	**latter**	**last**	順序上的先後

例 This bad situation became worse.
這種糟糕的情況變得更糟。

例 He wore the worst hat.
他戴著最糟糕的帽子。

例 Steak is a good choice, but lobster is better.
牛排是一個不錯的選擇，但龍蝦更好。

例 I know you're the best violinist.
我知道你是最好的小提琴手。

例 I have many kids. Please give me more candy.
我有很多孩子。請給我更多的糖果。

例 Ted always has the most toys.
泰德總是擁有最多的玩具。

例 We have much water. But we need more food.
我們有很多水。但是我們需要更多的食物。

例 My friend earned the most money.
我的朋友賺了最多的錢

例 Spring never comes late in this country.
這個國家的春天永遠不會遲到。

例 I will call you later.
我晚點再打給你。

例 The latest news shocked me.
最新的消息震驚我。(latest 表示時間上最晚發生，也就是最近或最新的意思)

例 I like the latter advice, not the former one.
我喜歡後面的建議，而不是前者。

注意： former是latter的相對詞——前一個。

例 It was his last day in the army.
這是他在軍隊的最後一天。

比較級 + than的用法

例 Nobody is younger than Jessica.
沒有人比傑西卡年輕。

例 My house is larger than this apartment.
我的房子比這間公寓大。

例 Your dog runs faster than hers.
你的狗跑得比她的狗快。

例 They have more customers than we do.
他們比我們有更多的客戶。(do取代have避免重複)

例 We won more championships than they did.
我們比他們贏了更多的冠軍。(did取代won避免重複，前面用過去式動詞won，後面也用過去式動詞did。)

最高級前面要加上 the

例 Mount Everest is the highest mountain in the world.
聖母峰是世界上最高的山峰。

例 This is the most expensive sweater in the store.
這是商店裡最昂貴的毛衣。

例 Lionel is the least annoying kid.
萊昂內爾是最不討人厭的孩子。

表示數量的形容詞（數量詞）

不可數	可數	兩者皆可
very **little** (很少) **a little** (一些) **much** (很多)	**very few** (很少) **a few** (一些) **Several** (一些) **many** (很多)	**any** (任何) **some** (一些) **a lot of** (很多) **lots of** (很多) **plenty of** (很多) **all** (全部)

例 Much time and money are spent on education.
大量時間和金錢用於教育。(兩個不可數名詞加起來有兩個種類，所以用are。)

例 Not many people came to the concert.
沒有多少人來參加音樂會。(people可數名詞)

例 There is a lot of sugar in candy.
糖果中有很多糖份。(sugar不可數名詞)

例 There are a lot of pupils who want to come.
有很多學生想來。(pupils可數名詞)

例 I have a few friends, but he has very few friends.
我有一些朋友，但他的朋友很少。

例 There are fewer customers theses days than last summer.
與去年夏天相比，這些天的客戶數量減少。(fewer是few的比較級)

例 Russel has little money, but Robert has less money.
羅素有很少的錢，但羅伯特錢更少。(less是little的比較級)

例 I had some rice for dinner.
我晚飯吃了一些米飯。(rice不可數名詞)

注意：通常any用在疑問句或否定句

例 Are there any problems with your career?
你的事業有任何問題嗎？

例 She doesn't want any gifts for Christmas.
她不想要任何聖誕節禮物。

例 I don't want any enemies.
我不想要任何敵人。

例 All the nurses respect this doctor.
所有護士都尊重這位醫生。

注意：all後面如果接代名詞，要用all of + 代名詞受格。

例 All you must attend this seminar. (✕)
All of you must attend this seminar. (✓)
你們所有人都必須參加這個研討會。

例 All us are celebrating! (✕)
All of us are celebrating! (✓)
我們都在慶祝！

every (每一)， each (每一)都用單數

例 Every shop was decorated with flowers. (每個商店都用鮮花裝飾。)
= All the shops were decorated with flowers. (所有商店都用鮮花裝飾。)

例 There was a gold medal in each competition. (每場比賽都有金牌。)
= There were prizes in all the competitions. (所有比賽都有金牌。)

注意：every 和 each前面不加the
We visit our daughter the every Christmas. (✕)
我們每個聖誕假期都會拜訪女兒。

數字 + times：幾倍

例 You earn four times his income.
你的收入是他的四倍。

the +形容詞的用法：這個種類的人

例 The rich must help the poor.
富人必須幫助窮人。(rich是形容詞：富有的，the rich：富人。poor是形容詞：貧窮的，the poor：窮人)
The elderly require special attention.
老人需要特別注意。(elderly是形容詞：年長的，the elderly：長者。)

與自己比較時，最高級前面不加 **the**

例 Taiwan is hottest in summer.
台灣在夏天最熱。

同時使用兩個相同的形容詞比較級

例 Everything is getting more and more expensive.
一切都變得越來越貴。

例 Grandma is looking older and older.
奶奶看起來越來越老。

形容詞比較級常見用法

例 The faster you drive, the more dangerous it is.
你開車越快，越危險。

例 The higher you climb, the harder you fall.
爬的越高，摔得越重。

數字的表達

阿拉伯數字	英文	第幾個（簡寫）	第幾個
1	one	1st	first
2	two	2nd	second
3	three	3rd	third
4	four	4th	fourth
5	five	5th	fifth
6	six	6th	sixth
7	seven	7th	seventh
8	eight	8th	eighth
9	nine	9th	ninth
10	ten	10th	tenth
11	eleven	11th	eleventh
12	twelve	12th	twelfth
13	thirteen	13th	thirteenth
14	fourteen	14th	fourteenth
15	fifteen	15th	fifteenth
16	sixteen	16th	sixteenth
17	seventeen	17th	seventeenth
18	eighteen	18th	eighteenth
19	nineteen	19th	nineteenth
20	twenty	20th	twentieth
21	twenty-one	21st	twenty-first
22	twenty-two	22nd	twenty-second
23	twenty-three	23rd	twenty-third
24	twenty-four	24th	twenty-fourth
30	thirty	30th	thirtieth
31	thirty-one	31st	thirty-first
40	forty	40th	fortieth
50	fifty	50th	fiftieth
100	one hundred	100th	hundredth
1,000	one thousand	1000th	thousandth

注意：第幾個前面要加the

例 He was the tenth President of the United States.
他是美國第十任總統。

例 It is the second time he went to Italy this year.
這是他今年第二次去意大利。

例 We are now in the 21st century.
我們現在在二十一世紀。

小數點與分數的唸法

小數點	唸法
0.5	**point five**
0.74	**point seven four**
0.08	**point zero eight**

分數	唸法
1/3	**one third**
3/4	**three fourths**
5/6	**five sixths**
1/2	**one half**
3/2	**three halves**

現在分詞當形容詞

前面章節曾提過現在分詞，也就是：動詞 + ing (V + ing)。現在分詞除了可用在現在進行式，也可當形容詞。

例 This film is so exciting!
這部電影是如此令人興奮！(excite是動詞：使人興奮，exciting變成形容詞。)

例 I found a very interesting article in the newspaper.
我在報紙上發現一篇非常有趣的文章。(interest是動詞：吸引或讓人感興趣，interesting變成形容詞，意思是：有趣的。)

例 The CEO shew up at the welcoming party.
執行長出席了歡迎派對。(welcome是動詞：歡迎，welcoming變成形容詞，意思是：歡迎的。)

名詞 + 現在分詞當形容詞

例 It is a heart-breaking news for Tina.
這對Tina是一個傷心的消息。

整句也可改成：

This news breaks Tina's heart.
這消息傷了Tina的心。

例 This roast fish is mouth-watering.
這條烤魚是令人垂涎的。

整句的意思就是：

This roast fish can water your mouth.
這條烤魚可以讓人口中充滿口水。

例 Australia is an English-speaking country.
澳大利亞是一個說英語的國家。

過去分詞可當形容詞

例 I am interested in this website.
我被這個網站吸引感興趣。

前面提到interest是動詞，意思是使人有興趣。Interested和interesting都可當形容詞，差別在現在分詞有主動的意思，而過去分詞有被動的意思。所以上面的句子也可改成：This website interests me.... 這個網站吸引我讓我感興趣。或者改成：This website is interesting to me.

再看一個範例。exhaust是動詞，意思是：使人精疲力竭。因此下面三個句子意思完全一樣。

例 The task exhausted him.
這個任務使他精疲力竭。(exhaust：動詞)

He was exhausted by the task.
他被這個任務弄得精疲力竭。(exhausted：過去分詞當形容詞)

For him, it was an exhausting task.
對他而言，這個任務是讓人精疲力竭的。(exhausting：現在分詞當形容詞)

hide 是動詞：隱藏，hidden是過去分詞：被隱藏。

例 Norman knows the hidden secret. (✓)
Norman knows the hiding secret. (✕)
諾曼知道隱藏的秘密。
秘密是被隱藏的，所以要用過去分詞當形容詞...hidden secret。

名詞 + 過去分詞當形容詞

例 I love this hand-picked tea.
我愛這親手採摘的茶。
(茶是被人採摘的，所以要用過去分詞picked，如果用現在分詞hand-picking就錯了。)

例 That pitcher is left-handed.
那投手是左撇子。

例 Tigers are four-legged animals.
老虎是四足動物。

請在(a) (b) (c) (d) 中選出正確答案（可能是複選）

1. I met ____.

   (a) a new someone (b) a someone new (c) new someone (d) someone new

2. Everything ____ fine.

   (a) is (b) was (c) are (d) were

3. Nobody is ____ than William.

   (a) smart (b) smarter (c) smartest (d) the smartest

4. That is an ____ story.

   (a) inspire (b) inspired (c) inspiring (d) inspires

5. We are living in the ____ century.

   (a) 21 (b) 21th (c) 21st (d) 21nd

6. Her father is getting ____.

   (a) old and old (b) older and older (c) oldest and oldest (d) old and older

7. He has ____ friends.

   (a) very little (b) very few (c) many (d) much

8. We have a lot of ____.

   (a) water (b) bread (c) tables (d) chairs

9. She doesn't like ____ mistakes.

   (a) some (b) any (c) all (d) all the

10. Vincent is ____ player.

    (a) strongest (b) the strongest (c) the most strongest (d) strong

1. (d) 形容詞new要放在someone後面，someone前面不加冠詞。
2. (a) (b) everything後面一定接單數動詞。
3. (b) than前面接形容詞比較級。
4. (b) (c) 現在分詞和過去分詞都可當形容詞，inspired表示被啓示的，inspiring表示啓示人的。
5. (c) 英文要講「第21個世紀」，所以是21st century。
6. (b) and前後接兩個形容詞比較級是常見文法，表示越來越….。
7. (b) (c) very few和many後面都可接可數名詞。
8. (a) (b) (c) (d) a lot of後面接可數名詞或不可數名詞。
9. (b) (d) doesn't中間有not，表示否定句，通常any用在否定句，而some用在肯定句。all the後面接名詞也是常見用法。
10. (b) 形容詞最高級前面加the，strongest已經是最高級，前面就不用most。

Part 8

副詞

副詞...可修飾動詞、形容詞、其它副詞、整個句子

前一章提到形容詞修飾名詞，例如：She lives in a big house. 用 big (大的)形容 house (房子)。

然而副詞卻不是修飾名詞，而是修飾動詞、形容詞、其它副詞、整個句子。我們以下將分別介紹。

副詞修飾動詞，副詞通常放在動詞之後

例 He speaks slowly.
他緩慢地說話。(副詞slowly修飾動詞speak)

例 The little girl can run quickly.
小女孩能跑得很快。(副詞quickly修飾動詞run)

例 Wilson drives carefully.
威爾遜小心地開車。(副詞carefully修飾動詞drive)

注意：但如果句子裡有受詞，副詞必須挪到受詞之後

例 He speaks Mandarin fluently. (副詞fluently放在受詞Mandarin後面)
他中文說得很流利。

例 He closed the door quietly. (副詞quietly放在受詞the door後面)
他靜靜地關了門。

副詞修飾形容詞

例 It's a very interesting topic.
這是一個非常有趣的話題。(副詞very修飾形容詞interesting)

例 They live in a newly painted room.
他們住在一個剛油漆好的房間裡。(副詞newly修飾形容詞painted，painted是過去分詞，前一章提到過去分詞可當形容詞。)

例 Joanna is really gorgeous.
喬安娜真的很漂亮。(副詞really修飾形容詞gorgeous)

注意：當副詞修飾形容詞時，通常放在被修飾的形容詞前面。

副詞修飾其它副詞

例 She addressed the board members very confidently.
她非常自信地向董事會成員發表了講話。(副詞very修飾副詞confidently)

例 She did it really well.
她做得很好。(副詞really修飾副詞well)

注意：當副詞修飾其他副詞時，通常放在被修飾的副詞前面。

副詞修飾整個句子

例 Obviously, a human being doesn't know everything.
顯然地，一個人類不會知道每件事情。(副詞obviously修飾整個句子)

例 Surprisingly, he solved this problem.
讓人驚訝地，他解決了這個問題。(副詞surprisingly修飾整個句子)

形容詞變副詞的常見方式	
形容詞	字尾 ＋ ly變副詞
quick (快的) **nice** (好的) **careful** (小心的) **anxious** (焦慮的) **beautiful** (美麗的) **slow** (慢的) **quiet** (安靜的) **recent** (最近的) **sudden** (忽然的)	**quickly** (快地) **nicely** (好地) **carefully** (小心地) **anxiously** (焦慮地) **beautifully** (美麗地) **slowly** (慢地) **quietly** (安靜地) **recently** (最近地) **suddenly** (忽然地)
有些形容詞字尾是**able**或**ible**	將**e**改成**y**變副詞
regrettable (遺憾的) **horrible** (可怕的) **capable** (有能力的) **gentle** (溫柔的) **possible** (可能的)	**regrettably** (遺憾地) **horribly** (可怕地) **capably** (有能力地) **gently** (溫柔地) **possibly** (可能地)
有些形容詞字尾是**y**	將**y**改成**ily**變副詞
happy (快樂的) **lucky** (幸運的) **easy** (容易的)	**happily** (快樂地) **luckily** (幸運地) **easily** (容易地)

注意：有些字雖然結尾是**ly**，卻是形容詞，而非副詞。
例如：**friendly** (友善的), **lovely** (可愛的), **lonely** (寂寞的), **neighbourly** (像鄰居的)

下列字形容詞與副詞相同	
形容詞	副詞
fast (快的)	**fast** (快地)
hard (難的)	**hard** (難地)
late (晚的)	**late** (晚地)
early (早的)	**early** (早地)
daily (每天的)	**daily** (每天地)

注意： lately (最近)也是副詞，意義和late (晚)不同。

例 Our tutor came to class late this morning.
我們老師今天早上上課遲到了。

例 Did you meet her lately?
你最近有沒有見到她？

形容詞與副詞完全不同	
形容詞	副詞
good (好的)	**well** (好地)

例 She's a good employee. She did it so well.
她是個好員工，她做得很好。(good是形容詞，用來修飾名詞employee。well是副詞，用來修飾動詞did。)

表示時間的副詞一般放在句尾，表示強調的時候可以放在句首。

注意：副詞不一定是單字，可以是由多個字所組成的副詞片語。例如：**at six o'clcok, at first, in the park...**等等。小單位的放前面，大單位的放後面。

例 I will meet you at eight o'clock tomorrow.
我明天八點跟你見面。

例 I want it now.
我現在就要它。

例 I played golf yesterday.
我昨天打高爾夫球。

例 I went there in June last year. (小單位的放前面，大單位的放後面)
我去年六月去了那裡。

例 Every year, millions of tourists visit here.
每年有數百萬遊客到這裡來。(強調每年，所以將Every year放在句首。)

例 The nurse checked his pulse once an hour.
護士每小時檢查他的脈搏一次。

注意：**once**是一次，**twice**是兩次，三次是**three times**，四次是**four times**，以此類推。

例 They gather here many times a month.
他們每個月在這裡聚集很多次。

例 He drives his stepfather to Fermont twice a year.
他每年兩次開車帶他的繼父去佛蒙特。

例 In Taiwan, most companies pay taxes yearly.
在台灣，大多數公司每年繳稅。(yearly = every year)

例 Her boss emails her weekly.
她的老闆每週發email給她。(weekly = every week)

其他類似的字還有：

Every day = daily (每天)

Every month = monthly (每月)

Every hour = hourly (每小時)

Every night = nightly (每晚)

Every quarter = quarterly (每季)

Every fortnight = fortnightly (每兩週)

表示地點的副詞一般放在句尾，表示強調的時候可以放在句首。

例 Don't put it there, put it here.
不要把它放在那裡，把它放在這裡。

例 My comb is here in my bag.
我的梳子在我的包裡。

例 Our children were playing upstairs.
我們的孩子們正在樓上玩耍。

例 It's so cold outside. We want to stay indoors.
外面很冷我們想留在室內

注意：everywhere每個地方，anywhere任何地方， somewhere某個地方，nowhere哪裡都不是。

例 They looked for Charles everywhere.
他們在每個地方尋找查爾斯。

例 There's a book shop somewhere downtown.
市中心某個地方有一家書店。

例 Did you go anywhere last night?
昨晚你去任何地方嗎？

注意：not anywhere = nowhere

例 I am not going anywhere. (我沒要去任何地方) = I am going nowhere. (我哪都不去)

事情發生頻率的副詞通常放在一般動詞前面，或be動詞後面。但如果是occasionally, sometimes, often, frequently, usually, regularly等字也可放在句首或句尾。

例 Fred usually goes to school by bus.
富萊德通常搭公車上學。

例 They are seldom home. (✓)
They seldom are home. (✕)
他們很少在家。(頻率副詞放在be動詞後面)

例 You're never home!
你永遠不在家！

例 Sometimes, they discipline those students.
有時，他們管教那些學生。

例 I miss my pal occasionally.
我偶爾想念我的朋友。

例 Always do your homework first!
一定要先做你的功課！

例 We sometimes dine in.
我們有時在家吃飯

例 They often go out for dinner.
他們經常出去吃飯。

例 I rarely see our principal.
我很少看到我們的校長。

例 She is always late for work.
她上班總是遲到。

例 Did he constantly lie?
他不斷說謊嗎？

例 Do you ever go to the opera house?
你去過歌劇院嗎？

例 These questions were frequently asked.
這些問題經常被問到。

例 That makeup room was normally occupied.
化妝室通常被佔用。

例 Both pen pals write to each other regularly.
兩個筆友都定期寫信給對方。

Still和already放在一般動詞前面，或be動詞後面。

例 They still love each other. They are still excited about the reunion.
他們仍然相愛。他們仍然很興奮這次重聚。

例 He already knew it.
他已經知道了

例 We're already late.
我們已經遲到了

enough 可當形容詞或副詞

例 You can't watch this program. You are not old enough.
你不能看這個節目。你年紀還不夠大。(enough當副詞)

例 We have enough money and enough time.
我們有足夠的錢和足夠的時間。 (enough當形容詞)

副詞when ...當…的時候

例 He joined chess club when he was at university.
他在大學時加入了棋藝社。

例 Everybody loves animation when they're kids.
每個人小時都喜歡動畫。

發生機率的副詞

Maybe 和 perhaps意思一樣，都是：或許。 通常放在句首。

例 Perhaps he understands.
也許他明白了。

例 Maybe it's a good choice.
也許這是一個不錯的選擇。

其他機率副詞放在一般動詞前面，或be動詞後面。

例 It is certainly not made of iron.
這當然不是鐵製的。

例 He can't possibly win the race.
他不可能贏得比賽。

例 That is probably the funniest joke.
這可能是最有趣的笑話。

例 This is definitely wrong.
這絕對是錯的。

動名詞也可當副詞修飾形容詞

前一章節提到動名詞可當形容詞修飾名詞，但如果將動名詞放在形容詞前面修飾形容詞，這個動名詞就變副詞。

例 The pizza is piping hot.
這披薩很熱。(piping修飾hot)

例 The weather is freezing cold in Toronto.
多倫多天氣寒冷。(freezing修飾 cold)

副詞的比較級和最高級

如同形容詞，副詞也有比較級和最高級，副詞的變化規則和形容詞的一樣。要注意，副詞的最高級可以不加 the。

規則變化中單音節和部分雙音節在字尾加 **er, est**

例 Diane works harder than Amy, but Severine works hardest in the office.
黛安比艾咪工作認真，但辦公室工作最認真的是莎弗琳。(harder：比較級，hardest：最高級)

例 Light travels faster than sound.
光速比音速快。

例 It's easier said than done.
說比做容易。

規則變化中三音節以上...前面加 **more, most, less, least**

例 Please handle this situation more carefully.
請更小心處理這個狀況。

例 The company operated less efficiently in 2007.
該公司在2007年運作效率較低。

例 What a shame! Katherine dance least gracefully.
多可惜！凱瑟琳舞蹈最不優雅。

例 She answered most politely.
她最禮貌地回答。

副詞的比較級和最高級...不規則變化

副詞	比較級	最高級
well (好地)	**better**	**best**
badly (糟糕地)	**worse**	**worst**

例 Charles can see better now.
查爾斯現在看得更清楚了

例 Gilbert looks best in that suit.
吉爾伯特穿那件西裝最好看。

例 Evan did the worst in the test.
伊凡在測試中做得最差。

副詞 **much** (更多)，**even** (甚至)，**a lot** (很多)，**far** (遠遠地)，**a little** (一些)，**slightly** (稍微)可修飾形容詞比較級或者副詞比較級。

例 Iron is much heavier than cotton.
鐵比棉花重得多。

例 Peter is good, but Paul is even better.
彼得是好的，但保羅甚至更好。

例 This is far nicer than that.
這遠比那好的多。

例 Things can become a lot more complicated.
事情可能變得更複雜許多。

例 She should speak a little more slowly.
她應該說得慢一點。

例 They move slightly faster now.
他們現在移動得稍微快一點。

注意：比較級前面不能用 **very** 修飾

例 Frank is a very worse competitor. (X)
弗蘭克是一個非常糟糕的競爭對手。

副詞 **also** (也)放在一般動詞前面，或 **be** 動詞後面。

例 I love spaghetti. I also love pizza.
我喜歡意大利麵條我也喜歡比薩。

例 I am also an athlete.
我也是一名運動員。

副詞 **too** 有兩個意思

1. 也 (放在句尾)

例 Jane plays the cello. Sam plays the cello, too.
珍拉大提琴。山姆也拉大提琴。

2. 太 (放在形容詞或副詞前面)

例 Don't drive too fast.
不要開太快。

例 You drank too much.
你喝太多了。

例 He has too many troubles.
他有太多的麻煩。

as + 形容詞 (或副詞) + **as**——跟…一樣

例 Michelle is as intelligent as Tracy.
蜜雪兒和崔西一樣聰明。

例 Tom is not as tall as this guy.
湯姆不像這個傢伙那麼高。

例 They have as many customers as we do.
他們和客戶一樣多。

例 Kim drinks as much juice as Steve.
金和史提夫喝了一樣多的果汁。

as fast as possible (速度儘快**)**，**as soon as possible (**時間儘快**)**

例 He swam as fast as possible.
他盡可能游得快。

例 Please come here asap.
請儘快來這裡。(asap = as soon as possible)

副詞 + 分詞也是很常見的形容詞

副詞 + 現在分詞 **(Ving)** 作為形容詞

例 Hard-working (勤奮認真的) , fast-growing (快速成長的)

副詞 + 過去分詞 **(p.p.)** 作為形容詞

例 newly-built (新蓋的), well-known (廣為人知的)

練習題

請在(a) (b) (c) (d) 中選出正確答案（可能是複選）

1. She speaks ____

   (a) fast (b) slow (c) slowly (d) fluent

2. It's a very ____ story.

   (a) interestingly (b) interesting (c) beautiful (d) beautifully

3. Sam did it ____.

   (a) very good (b) so good (c) very well (d) so well

4. I flew to Canada ____.

   (a) in May last year (b) last year May (c) May last year (d) in last year May

5. ____ good.

   (a) It's maybe (b) It maybe is (c) Maybe it's

   (d) It maybe is not

6. It's ____ better than that.

   (a) much (b) far (c) a little (d) a lot

7. Seattle is ____ than Taipei.

   (a) colder (b) very colder (c) even colder (d) colder even

8. I ____ happy.

   (a) also am (b) am also (c) also be (d) also am not

9. 何者正確？

   (a) I am young enough (b) I am enough young (c) She has enough water (d) She has water enough

10. Cherry is ____.

(a) gently (b) friendly (c) lovely (d) lonely

1. (a) (c) speaks是一般動詞，後面接副詞。
2. (b) (c) story是名詞，前面加形容詞。
3. (c) (d) did是一般動詞，後面接副詞well。
4. (a) May前面要加介係詞in，時間單位小的放前面，大的放後面，所以May放在last year前面。
5. (c) maybe放句首。
6. (a) (b) (c) (d) 四個都可以修飾形容詞比較級。
7. (a) (c) 形容詞比較級前面可用even，但不能用very修飾。
8. (b) also放在be動詞後面。 (d) 錯在also不可用在否定句，我也不快樂要用I am not happy, either.
9. (a) (c) enough放在形容詞後面，或名詞前面。
10. (b) (c) (d) be動詞後面用形容詞來形容主詞，gently是副詞。

Part 9

動詞進階觀念

動名詞

動名詞是動詞的變形...變成了名詞。動名詞是以原形動詞 + ing 所構成，簡稱 V + ing。動名詞和現在分詞長的完全一樣，都是V + ing。

例如動詞learn的動名詞就是learning。動詞work的動名詞就是working。可以放名詞的地方都可以放動名詞。

例 Walking is a good exercise.
步行是一項很好的運動。(動名詞Walking當主詞，因為是第三人稱單數，所以後面的 be動詞是is。)

例 Writing is more difficult than reading. (✓)
Write is more difficult than read. (✕)
寫作比閱讀更困難。(動詞不能當成名詞使用，所以Write和 read要改成動名詞)

例 Listening to music makes me happy.
聽音樂讓我很開心。(動名詞 Listening加上to music變成動名詞片語當主詞，後面一般動詞是單數 makes。)

有些動詞後面可加動名詞

例 He enjoys taking a walk.
他喜歡散步。

例 He enjoys not working.
他喜歡不必工作。(動名詞前面直接加not表示否定)

例 Keep learning English!
持續學習英文！

例 Lucy practices playing the piano every day.
璐西每天練習彈鋼琴。

例 I can't help thinking about its face.
我忍不住想到了它的臉。(can't help是一個片語：忍不住)

例 I can smell something burning.
我可以聞到有東西燃燒。

例 I heard someone singing a lullaby.
我聽到有人在唱搖籃曲。

例 I saw her standing there.
我看見她站在那裡。

例 Helen sat there wondering.
海倫坐在那裡納悶著。

英文中常看到go + 動名詞，這種用法表示去參加某種活動。

例 Wilson went skating last week.
威爾遜上週去滑冰。

例 Do you want to go skiing with me?
你想和我一起去滑雪嗎？

例 Alan doesn't go fishing on Sunday.
艾倫星期天不去釣魚。

be 動詞的動名詞是being

例 I was interrupted.
我被插話了。

例 I don't like being interrupted.
我不喜歡被插話。(like 後面接動名詞，was 改成 being。)

常見的動詞片語 + 動名詞

例 I am lonely. But I don't mind being lonely. (✓)
I am lonely. But I don't mind am lonely. (✕)
我寂寞。但我不介意寂寞。(don't mind是動詞片語：不介意，後面接動名詞，am改成being。)

例 They had no difficulty finding the spot.
他們毫無困難找到這個地點。(have no difficulty是動詞片語：無困難。)

例 Alex finally gave up smoking.
亞歷克斯終於放棄了吸煙。(give up是動詞片語：放棄。)

例 He kept on asking for help.
他一直在尋求幫助。(keep on是動詞片語：持續。)

介係詞 + 動名詞 (介係詞後面只能接名詞，不能接動詞，所以將動詞改成動名詞)

例 Please have lunch with me before leave. (✕)
Please have lunch with me before leaving. (✓)

請在離開前和我一起吃午飯。(介係詞before + 動名詞leaving)

例 She is good at painting.
她善於畫畫。

例 He learns English grammar by listening to the radio.
他藉由聽收音機學習英文文法。

例 He is thinking about studying abroad.
他正在考慮去國外留學。

例 That physicist is capable of winning a Nobel prize.
那個物理學家有能力贏得諾貝爾獎。

動名詞可修飾前面的名詞

例 There were seven people waiting for the bus.
有七個人在等車。(動名詞waiting修飾前面的名詞七個人)

例 The boy talking to Angel is her roommate.
那個和安琪說話的男孩是她的室友。(動名詞talking修飾boy)

例 I found the pizza boy sitting outside. (動名詞sitting修飾pizza boy)
我發現送披薩的男孩坐在外面。

例 The guy standing at the door is Donald.
站在門口的那個男孩是唐納。(動名詞standing修飾guy)

常見句型：虛擬主詞It ＋ 形容詞 ＋ 動名詞來引導一個句子

例 It's great living in freedom. = Living in freedom is great.
生活在自由中是很棒的。

例 It's terrible behaving this way. = Behaving this way is terrible.
這種行為方式是可怕的。

例 It's disgusting listening to his remarks. =Listening to his remarks is disgusting.
聽他的言論讓人作嘔。

例 It is sad hearing you're not coming the next week. = Hearing you're not coming the next week is sad.
聽到你不來讓人悲傷。（前一種說法較常見，因為第二種說法主詞太長了。）

不定詞

不定詞是以 to ＋ 原形動詞所構成，簡稱to ＋ V。不定詞和動名詞一樣，都是動詞的變形...變成了名詞。

動詞learn的不定詞就是to learn。動詞work的不定詞就是to work。

注意：前面提過to是介係詞，後面接名詞或動名詞。例如：She went to Chicago. (她去芝加哥。)

然而在不定詞用法中to是副詞，後面接動詞原型。

例 To know her is to love her. (✓)
Know her is love her. (✗) (know和love都是動詞，不能當名詞使用。)
了解她就是愛她。

用It is 當主詞的用法比上面不定詞當主詞的句型更常見。

例 To become a dancer is my dream. (✓) (用不定詞當主詞)
It is my dream to become a dancer. (✓) (用It當主詞)
Becoming a dancer is my dream. (✓) (用動名詞當主詞)
成為舞者是我的夢想。

例 To understand Chemistry is our goal. (✓) (用不定詞當主詞)
Understanding Chemistry is our goal. (✓) (用動名詞當主詞)

It is our goal to understand Chemistry. (✓) (用It當主詞)
了解化學是我們的目標。

有些動詞後面會接不定詞

例 I want to study Spanish.
我想學西班牙語。

例 We invited them to join us.
我們邀請他們加入我們。

例 She agreed to help him.
她同意幫助他。

例 He chose to stay at home.
他選擇留在家裡。。

例 He failed to convince him.
他沒能說服他。

例 She intends to write an autobiography.
她打算寫一本自傳。

例 She hopes to be elected president.
她希望被選為總統。(to + be + 過去分詞elected：被動式用法)

例 The carpet needs to be washed.
地毯需要被洗滌。(to + be + 過去分詞washed：被動式用法)

不定詞的否定前面直接加not

例 I decided not to go to London.
我決定不去倫敦。

例 He asked me not to be late.
他要我不要遲到。

例 The most important thing is not to give up.
最重要的事情是不要放棄。

常見用法：名詞接不定詞

例 I need something to eat.
我需要吃東西。

例 This is the right thing to do.
這是正確該做的事情。

例 It was a good decision to call him.
打電話給他是一個很好的決定。

例 His wish to become a diver was well known.
他想成為潛水員的願望是眾所周知的。

例 Larry's desire to improve impressed me.
賴瑞的改善願望讓我印象深刻。

例 His advice to build a highway was popular.
他建造高速公路的建議受歡迎。

例 Her attempt to change them was unsuccessful.
她試圖改變他們是不成功的。

例 The decision to increase taxes was not welcome.
增加稅收的決定是不受歡迎的。

常見用法：be動詞 + 形容詞接不定詞

例 Noah was delighted to receive such good feedback.
諾亞很高興收到這樣好的反饋。

例 He is lucky to have such a girlfriend.
他很幸運有這樣一個女朋友。

例 I'm pleased to meet you.
我很高興見到你。

例 Dorothy is old enough to make up her own mind.
桃樂茜年紀夠大，可以自己決定。

例 I'm disappointed to hear that you blew it.
我很失望聽到你搞砸了。

例 They were careful not to look proud.
他們小心不要讓自己看起來驕傲。

例 It is good of you to assist me.
你幫助我真好。(類似的說法還有It's nice of you to + 動詞，或者It's kind of you to + 動詞)

例 It is important for May to be patient.
對梅而言有耐心很重要。

下列用法中 **to** 表示：為了…

例 You need to exercise more to lose weight.
為了減肥你需要更多運動。

例 He works hard to earn the respect of his coworkers.
他努力工作為了贏得他同事的尊重。

例 Jasmine sold everything to get the money that she needed.
茉莉花出售一切為了獲得她需要的錢。

例 David uses goodenglish.com to learn English.
大衛使用goodenglish.com這個網站學習英語。

too + 形容詞 + **to** + 動詞**...**-此用法表示太…以致於不能…

例 You are too young to watch this program.
你太年輕了，不能看這個節目。

例 It's too good to be true!
好得不真實！

例 He is too weak to walk.
他虛弱到不能走路。

下列用法中，動詞後面加動名詞或不定詞的意義幾乎相同。

例 She continued talking. = She continued to talk.
她繼續說話。

例 He hates watching soap operas. = He hates to watch soap operas.
他討厭看肥皂劇。

例 Samantha likes reading. = Samantha likes to read.
薩曼莎喜歡讀書。

例 He prefers taking a shower at night. = He prefers to take a shower at night.
他喜歡晚上洗澡。

例 George is afraid to fly. = George is afraid of flying.
喬治怕坐飛機。

例 I started to learn gardening since 2016. = I started learning gardening since 2016.
自2016年以來我開始學園藝。

下列用法中，動詞後面加動名詞或不定詞的意義完全不同。

例 I stopped smoking.
我停止吸菸。(已經戒菸了)

例 I stopped to smoke a cigarette.
我停下來吸根菸。(還在吸菸)

例 I remember telling him.
我記得告訴過他。(已經說了)

例 I must remember to tell him.
我應該要記得告訴他。(還沒說)

例 I forgot to feed my parrot.
我忘了餵鸚鵡。

例 I forgot feeding my parrot.
我忘了已經餵過鸚鵡。

連綴動詞

第八章副詞曾提到動詞後面接副詞。例如：He walks quietly.（他靜靜地走。），這裡的副詞quietly修飾動詞walk。

然而連綴動詞後面不接副詞，而是接形容詞來修飾主詞。

例 Kent looks happy.
肯特看起來很開心。（這裡的look是連綴動詞，後面接形容詞happy。）

例 Kent looked at the photo happily.
肯特高興地看著照片。（這裡的look是一般動詞，後面接副詞happily。）

由此可知同一動詞可能有兩種不同用法。

例 This chicken tastes delicious.
這雞肉嚐起來可口。（這裡的taste是連綴動詞，後面接形容詞delicious。）

例 They tasted the chicken.
他們品嚐了雞肉。（這裡的taste是一般動詞）

例 The tea smells good. (✓)
The tea smells well. (✕)
茶聞起來很棒。（這裡的smell是連綴動詞，後面接形容詞good，well是副詞。）

例 Sally grew angry.
莎莉生氣了。(grow是連綴動詞，後面接形容詞angry。)

例 Some kids grow faster.
有些孩子長得更快。(grow是一般動詞。)

例 Your plans sound nice.
你的計劃聽起來不錯。（sound是連綴動詞，後面接形容詞nice）

例 Sometimes, kids act foolish.
有時，孩子們會行為愚蠢。（在這裡act是連綴動詞，後面接形容詞foolish。）

例 He acted in three plays.
他在三齣戲中演出。（在這裡act是一般動詞。）

時態

前面已介紹過現在式、過去式等時態。現在介紹英文中其他時態。

時態主題一：未來式

未來式用在表示未來的動作，不管主詞是第幾人稱、單複數，動詞前面都加助動詞will。

例 I will paint my house green.
我將把我的房子漆成綠色。
縮寫方式：I will = I'll, we will = we'll, You will = You'll, he will = He'll, she will = she'll, they will = they'll, it will通常沒縮寫。

否定句 **will not = won't**

例 I won't forget this. = I will not forget this.
我將不會忘記這事。

疑問句將 **will** 或 **won't** 放在句首

例 Will you give me a hand?
你會幫我嗎？

例 Won't you go to the party?
你不去參加派對嗎？

注意：如果句中有**when, while, before, after, as soon as**等時間副詞連接句子，則時間副詞後面的句子不可用未來式。

例 I'll come home when I finish work.
完成工作後我將回家。(雖然完成工作是未來的事，但不可用when I will finish work)

例 I'll attend your church while I am in Oregon. (✓)
I'll attend your church while I will be in Oregon. (✕)
當我在俄勒岡州時，我會出席你的教會。

例 Now I'm 22. I will travel to Africa before I turn 25. (✓)
Now I'm 22. I will travel to Africa before I will turn 25. (✕)
我現在22。在25歲之前，我將前往非洲。

例 She will invite you to her home after you return from Tokyo.
從東京回來後，她會邀請你回家。

例 Harry will go to your place as soon as you text him.
一旦你給他發簡訊，哈利就會去你的地方。

主動式與被動式

例 Eric's parents will send him to school.
艾瑞克的父母將會送他上學。

例 Eric will be sent to school by his parents.
艾瑞克將被父母送到學校。(此句是被動式，第二章提過被動式的型態是：be動詞 + 過去分詞，所以未來式的被動式的型態是：will + be + 過去分詞。)

例 Someone will finish the course by 5:00 PM.
有人將在下午5點之前完成課程。

例 The course will be finished by 5:00 PM.
課程將在下午5:00完成。(基本上此句與上一句意思一樣，唯一差別是第一句是主動式，第二句是被動式)

例 The new chef will cook the dinner.
新廚師將煮晚餐。（主動式）

例 The dinner will be cooked by the new chef.
晚餐將由新廚師來煮。（被動式）

例 Someone will replace the manager.
有人將取代經理。（主動式）

例 The manager will be replaced.
經理將被取代。（被動式）

時態主題二：現在進行式

現在進行式用來強調此刻正在發生的事

肯定句型態是：be動詞現在式 ＋ 現在分詞。 現在分詞就是一般動詞+ing (簡稱Ving)。

例 I'm laughing.
我正在笑

例 Please be quiet. The children are sleeping.
請安靜。孩子們正在睡覺

例 They are reading their books.
他們正在讀書。

例 It's raining.
正在下雨。

例 I'm looking for a new apartment.
我正在尋找一個新的公寓。

否定句型態是：be動詞 ＋ not ＋ 現在分詞

例 I'm not sleeping.
我不是在睡覺。

例 You are not watching TV.
你沒在看電視。

疑問句型態是：將肯定句的be動詞移到主詞前面

例 Am I dreaming?
我在做夢嗎？

例 Is he standing?
他站著嗎？

例 Is Tammy running?
Tammy在跑步嗎？

Yes, she is. (No, she isn't.)
是的，她在跑步。（不，她不是在跑步。）

有些動詞不能用進行式

例 He is wanting to buy a new car. (✕)
He wants to buy a new car. (✓)
他想買一輛新車。(want不能用進行式)

例 She has three dogs and a cat. (✓)
She's having three dogs and a cat. (✕)
她有三隻狗和一隻貓。(have的意思是：擁有。不能用進行式)

例 She's having supper. (✓)
她正在吃晚餐。(這裡have的意思是：吃。可用進行式)

例 I can see Anthony in the garden. (✓)
我在花園裡看到安東尼。

例 I'm seeing Anthony in the garden. (✕)
我正在花園裡看到安東尼。(see的意思是：看。不能用進行式)

例 I'm seeing Anthony later. (✓)
我等會和安東尼見面。(see的意思是：會面。可用進行式)

例 I am seeing her. (✓)
我在和她約會。(see的意思是：和某人約會。可用進行式)

有時現在進行式並非表示現在正在做的事，而是表示計畫未來要做的事

例 I'm meeting Jim at the airport.
我將在機場會見吉姆。

例 I am leaving tomorrow.
我明天將離開。

例 Tina is starting university in September.
蒂娜9月將開始上大學。

例 I'm playing football tomorrow.
我明天將踢足球。

例 He's picking me up at the airport.
他將到機場接我。

be動詞 + going to + 動詞原型表示未來將做某件事情

注意：**going to**常簡稱**gonna**，通常在口語中才出現。

例 She is not going to spend her money on this hat.
她不會把錢花在這頂帽子上。

例 They're going to move to LA.
他們要搬到洛杉磯

例 Aren't we going to watch football game?
我們不是要看足球比賽嗎？

例 Is it gonna rain?
要下雨了嗎？

現在進行式的被動式：**be** 動詞 + **being** + 過去分詞

例 Tom is writing the letter. (主動式)
The letter is being written by Tom. (被動式)
湯姆正在寫信。(雖然中文不會說：信正在被湯姆寫，但英文有這種用法。)

例 Your room is being cleaning right now. (✕)
Your room is being cleaned right now. (✓)
您的房間正在清理。(被動式要用過去分詞cleaned)

例 Nana is preparing the feast.
娜娜正在準備盛宴。(主動式)

例 The feast is being prepared.
盛宴正在準備中。(被動式...不須強調是娜娜或任何其他人準備的)

時態主題三：過去進行式

過去進行式用來表示過去某時段正在進行的動作
肯定句型態是：be動詞過去式 + 現在分詞，否定句加not。

例 I was walking in the snow.
我正在雪地裡散步。

例 Last night at 8 PM, I wasn't eating dinner with Jacqueline.
昨晚8點，我沒有和杰奎琳一起吃飯。

例 Richard was watching television while Eddie was reading.
當艾迪正在讀書的時候，理察正在看電視。

疑問句將be動詞放在句首

例 Was she studying at noon?
她中午在學習嗎？

例 Weren't you playing cards when I came in?
我進來時你們不是在玩牌嗎？

例 Were you listening while he was talking?
你在說話的時候他有在聽嗎？

過去進行式的被動式：be動詞過去式 + being + 過去分詞

例 The waiter was serving appetizers.
服務員正在上開胃菜。(主動式)

例 The appetizers were being served by the waiter.
開胃菜正被服務員上菜。(被動式...雖然中文這樣說怪怪的，但英文可這樣用。)

be動詞過去式 + going to + 動詞原型表示過去時間有計畫將在未來做某件事情

例 Last Friday we were going to tidy the basement the next day.
上週五我們打算第二天要整理地下室。

例 She was going to give me a lift when you saw her yesterday.
昨天當你看到她時，她正準備載我一程。

例 Her boss was going to make an job offer to me.
她的老闆正準備要給我工作機會。(主動式)

例 I was going to be made a job offer by her boss.
我將被她的老闆給一個工作機會。(被動式...雖然中文這樣說怪怪的，但英文可這樣用。)

時態主題四：未來進行式

未來進行式：未來某時間將正在進行某件事情
肯定句型態是：will + be動詞 + 現在分詞，否定句will後面加not，疑問句將will放在句首。

例 I will be watching NBA finals game7 next Sunday evening.
下個星期天晚上我將正在看NBA總決賽第七戰。

例 This time next week I won't be delivering your goods.
下星期這個時間我不會正在遞送你的貨物。

例 Will I be sleeping in this room 5 hours later?
5小時後我會在這個房間睡覺嗎？

注意：時間副詞**when**後面的句子不可用未來式

例 I will be waving at you when your bus arrives. (✓)
I will be waving at you when your bus will arrive. (✕)
當你的巴士到達時我會向你招手。

未來進行式的被動式：**will + be + being** + 過去分詞

例 At 7PM tonight, I promise I will be washing the dishes.
今晚下午七點，我保證會正在洗碗。(主動式)

例 At 7PM tonight, the dishes will be being washed by me. You can take my word for it.
今晚下午七點，碗將正在被我洗。你可以相信我的話。(被動式)

時態主題五：現在完成式

形式：複數主詞...have ＋ 過去分詞。單數主詞...has ＋ 過去分詞。

肯定句：I have seen him.
否定句：I have not seen him.
疑問句：Have I seen him?
簡寫：I have = I've, you have = you've, we have = we've, they have = they've, he has = he's

注意： he has和he is的簡寫都是He's，she has和she is的簡寫都是she's，所以要從前後文判斷是哪一個。

A Have you told Jack?
你已經告訴傑克？

B Yes, I have/No I haven't.
是的，我有/不，我沒有。

現在完成式：從過去就開始，現在仍然如此。

例 I have lived in Germany since 2005.
自2005年以來我一直住在德國。

例 Martha has loved Chinese food since she was 13.
13歲以後，瑪莎一直愛中國菜。

例 He has become my best friend.
他已經成為我最好的朋友。

現在完成式也可表示：到現在為止已經完成的事情

例 I have had 6 tests this month.
我本月已經有了6次測驗。

例 He has made me glad.
他已經使我開心。

例 So far, Darren has only found a job.
到目前為止，達倫只找到了一份工作。

例 I have been to Vancouver three times.
我已經去過溫哥華三次。(我目前不在溫哥華)

例 She's gone to Vancouver for 3 week.
她已經去了溫哥華3週。(她目前人在溫哥華)

注意： **been to**是去過但目前不在那裏。**gone to**是已經去了，目前在那裏。

ever（曾經）和never（不曾）放在過去分詞前面

例 Have you ever eaten kimchi?
你曾經吃過泡菜嗎？

例 She has never said that to me before.
她不曾對我說過那種話。

already放在過去分詞前面，或句子最後。

例 They have been to Osaka already.
他們已經去過大阪。

例 Have you already written to Jimmy?
你已經寫信給吉米了嗎？

yet (尚未)放在句子最後

例 They haven't eaten yet.
他們還沒吃飯。

現在完成式強調到目前為止，所以一定用現在的時間，不會使用過去的時間。

例 I have noticed the sign yesterday. (✕)
I have noticed the sign now. (✓)
我已經注意到這個記號了。

例 We have just bought a new car.
我們已經剛買了一輛新車。(✓)

例 We have just bought a new car last week. (✕) (現在完成式，不會使用過去的時間。)

注意：若是過去的時間已經完成的事，則用過去完成式。下一單元會提到。

過去式強調以往發生但現在並非如此，而現在完成式包括現在此刻。

例 We spoke to Edward yesterday.
我們昨天跟愛德華說過話。(過去式：現在沒說了)

例 Ivy took a selfie two minutes ago.
愛薇兩分鐘前自拍。(過去式：現在沒有)

例 He has taught me about Accounting for 6 months.
他已經教我6個月會計學。(現在完成式：到目前為止六個月，表示現在可能還在教)

例 He taught me about Accounting 6 months ago.
他6個月前教我會計學。(過去式：現在沒教了)

last year 指去年， in the last year指過去一年中。last month 指上個月， in the last month指過去一個月中。

例 I went to Mexico last year.
去年我去了墨西哥。(過去式)

例 Have you heard from him in the last year?
過去一年中你聽到過他的消息嗎？ (現在完成式)

例 I have seen this episode 3 times in the last month.
我過去一個月看了這個劇集3次。(現在完成式)

例 I saw this episode last month.
我上個月看到這個劇集。(過去式)

現在完成式被動式：have或has ＋ been ＋ 過去分詞

例 Many tourists have visited that castle.
許多遊客已經參觀了那座城堡。(主動式)

例 That castle has been visited by many tourists. (✓)
That castle have been visited by many tourists. (✕)
那個城堡已經被許多遊客參觀過了。(被動式，主詞是第三人稱單數That castle，所以用has，不用have。)

例 I have kept all your old letters.
我已經保留了你所有的舊信件。(主動式)

例 All your old letters have been kept.
你所有的舊信件都被保留下來了。(被動式)

例 Tammy has booked a flight for her hubby.
Tammy已經為她的丈夫訂了航班。（主動式）

例 A flight has been booked for Tammy's hubby.
一個航班已經為Tammy的丈夫預訂了。（被動式）

例 The manager has changed lock for you.
經理已經為了你換鎖。

例 The lock has been changed for you by the manager.
為了你，鎖已經被經理換了。

時態主題六：過去完成式

形態：had ＋ 過去分詞

肯定句：I had said.

否定句：I had not said. = I hadn't said.

疑問句：Had I said?

疑問句回答：Yes, I had. No, I hadn't.

例 I had = I'd, you had = you'd, he had = he'd, she had = she'd, we had = we'd, it had = it'd

過去完成式：過去某個時間點以前就已經完成的事。過去時間點用過去式，之前已完成的事用過去完成式。

例 They had had lunch when the teacher called the roll. (✓)
They have had lunch when the teacher called the roll. (✕)
當老師點名時，他們已經吃了午餐。(老師點名用過去式，已經吃了午餐用過去完成式)

例 Petty passed the exam in July because she had studied very hard for 3 years.
Petty七月通過了考試，因為之前她已經辛苦研讀三年。(通過考試用過去式，已經辛苦研讀三年用過去完成式)

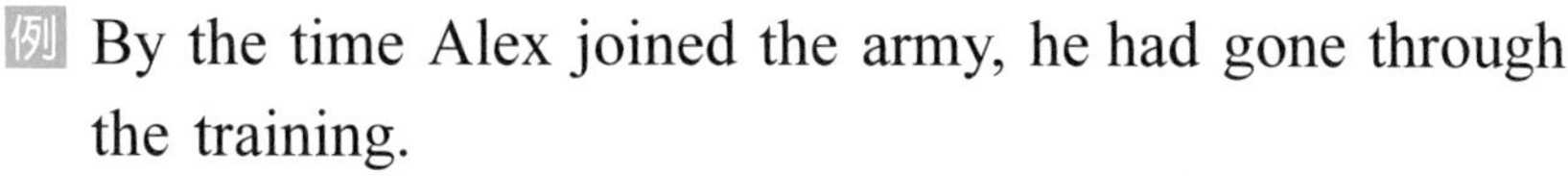

例 By the time Alex joined the army, he had gone through the training.
當亞歷克斯加入軍隊時，他已經歷了訓練。(加入軍隊用過去式，已經歷了訓練用過去完成式)

過去完成式的被動式：had + been + 過去分詞

例 Someone had opened the door before they arrived.
他們在到達之前有人已經打開了門。(主動式)

例 The door had been opened before they arrived.
他們到達之前門已經被打開了。(被動式)

例 Dwight had been taught a precious lesson before that.
在此之前，德懷特已經被教了一個寶貴的功課。(被動式)

時態主題七：未來完成式

未來完成式：描述未來某時間點將完成的事

形態：will have + 過去分詞，或者：be動詞 + going to + have + 過去分詞。

肯定句：I will have boarded the plane.
我將已經登機了。

否定句：I will not have boarded the plane.

疑問句： will I have boarded the plane?

例 I won't have finished this task by the end of August.
8月底我不會已經完成這項工作。

例 I will have been here for six months on January 23rd.
1月23日時我將已經在這裡待六個月。

例 Will you have eaten when I pick you up?
當我接你的時候你會已經吃完飯了嗎？

例 Will they have revised the manual by 5:00 tomorrow?
他們明天5點之前會修改完手冊嗎？

注意：現在完成式、過去完成式、未來完成式的差別在於動作完成的時間點。

例 It's May 1st now. I have earned USD30,000 since April 22nd.
現在是5月1日。我從4月22日至今已經賺了30,000美元。(現在完成式)

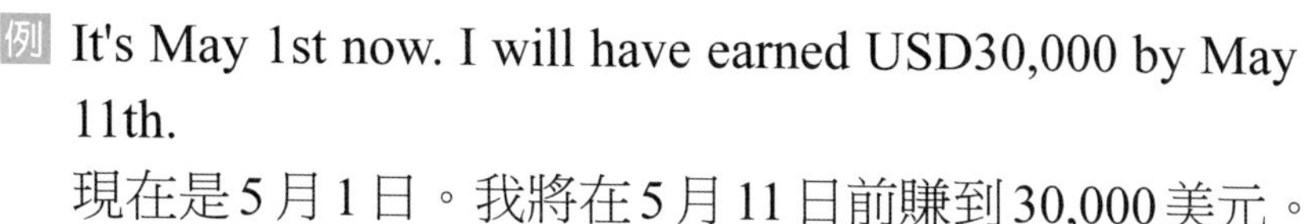

例 It's May 1st now. I will have earned USD30,000 by May 11th.
現在是5月1日。我將在5月11日前賺到30,000美元。(未來完成式)

例 It's May 1st now. I had earned USD30,000 when you saw me on April 22nd.
現在是5月1日。4月22日你見到我時，我已經賺了30,000美元。(過去完成式)

注意：如同前面未來式提到的，**by the time, before, when, while**等時間副詞後面句子不可加**will**。

例 She is going to have watered indoor plants by the time you get home. (✓)
She is going to have watered indoor plants by the time you will get home. (✕)
當你回家的時候，她將已經替室內植物澆完水。

例 Will you have learned enough French before you go to Paris next month? (✓)
Will you have learned enough French before you will go to Paris next month? (✕)
在你下個月去巴黎之前，你會已經學到足夠的法語嗎？

未來完成式被動式：will have been + 過去分詞

例 Tony will have completed the project before the deadline.
Tony將在截止日期前完成專案。(主動式)

例 The project will have been completed by Tony before the deadline.
專案將在截止日期前被Tony完成。(被動式)

例 Tony is going to have completed the project before the deadline.
Tony將在截止日期前完成專案。(主動式)

例 The project is going to have been completed by Tony before the deadline.
專案將在截止日期前被Tony完成。(被動式)

時態主題八：現在完成進行式

過去就開始，現在仍進行中的行動。

形態：Have或has + been + 現在分詞

肯定句：He has been pondering about it.

他一直在思考它。

否定句：He has not been pondering about it.

疑問句：Has he been pondering about it?

比起現在完成式，現在完成進行式更強調動作仍在進行中。

例 Alice has felt some hostility.
愛麗絲已經感到有些敵意。(現在完成式)

例 Alice has been feeling some hostility.
愛麗絲已經感到有些敵意。(現在完成進行式...強調此刻仍能感到敵意)

例 We have been standing in line for over 3 hours!
我們已經排隊超過3個小時！(現在完成進行式...強調此刻仍在排隊)

現在完成進行式很少使用被動式，所以不舉例。

時態主題九：過去完成進行式

過去某件事情發生前，就已持續一段時間的事件。

形態：had ＋ been ＋ 現在分詞

肯定句：He had been working when his mom called.

他媽媽打電話來時他一直在工作。

否定句：He had not been working when his mom called.

疑問句：Had he been working when his mom called?

例 That thug had been yelling at him when the police came.
當警察來時，那個惡棍已經一直對他吼叫。

例 Lisa lost 20kg because she had been exercising regularly for months.
麗莎減重20公斤因為當時她已經規律運動幾個月。

例 His voice was so hoarse because he was singing too loud.
他的聲音很嘶啞，因為他正在唱得太大聲了。(過去進行式...表示他當時正在大聲唱歌導致聲音很嘶啞)

例 His voice was so hoarse because he had been singing too loud.
他的聲音很嘶啞，因為他已經唱得太大聲了。(過去完成進行式...表示他當時已經大聲唱歌一陣子，導致聲音很嘶啞)

過去完成進行式很少使用被動式，所以不舉例。

時態主題十：未來完成進行式

形態：will have ＋ been ＋ 現在分詞

肯定句：I will have been waiting here for 2 hours by 6pm.
下午6點時我將已經在這裡等了兩個小時。

否定句：I won't have been waiting here for 2 hours by 6pm.

疑問句：Will I have been waiting here for 2 hours by 6pm?

Will 也可改成 **be** 動詞 **+ going to**

肯定句：You are going to have been waiting here for 2 hours by 6pm.
下午6點時你將已經在這裡等了兩個小時。

疑問句：Are you going to have been waiting here for 2 hours by 6pm?

否定句：You are not going to have been waiting here for 2 hours by 6pm.

例 When I finish my lunch, I will have been eating for 3 hours.
當我吃完午餐時，我將已經吃了3個小時。

例 When the alarm clock wakes me up tomorrow morning, I will have been sleeping for 11 hours.
當鬧鐘明天早上叫醒我時，我將已經睡了11個小時。
未來完成進行式很少使用被動式，所以不舉例。

助動詞

顧名思義助動詞的用途就是輔助說明動詞。助動詞的特性...後面永遠不加s或ing，前面也不加to。助動詞後面永遠接動詞原型。常見的助動詞有can, may, could, might, should等等。

表示能力的助動詞有 **can** 和 **could**，其中 **can** 表示現在或將來有能力做某件事情。

例 He can swim like a fish.
他可以像魚一樣游泳。

例 They can't dance very well.
他們無法將舞跳得好。(can't = cannot)

例 Can you ride a bike?
你會騎自行車嗎？ (疑問句將助動詞放在句首)

Yes, I can/ No I can't.

是的，我可以/不，我不能。

例 Can't you understand this joke?
你不明白這個笑話嗎？

例 She can speaks several languages. (X) (助動詞can後面須接原型動詞speak，即使She是第三人稱單數，speak也不加s。)

例 She cans speak several languages. (X) (助動詞永遠不加s，即使She是第三人稱單數。)

例 She can speak several languages. (✓)
她可以說幾種語言。

例 I teach her to can speak several languages. (X)
我教她可以說幾種語言。(助動詞前面永遠不加to)

Could 是 **can** 的過去式，表示過去有能力做某件事情。

例 She couldn't get a job in silicon valley last year.
她去年在矽谷找不到工作。(couldn't = could not)

例 I could do 100 pushups in my twenties.
我二十多歲的時候可以在做100個俯地挺身。

could have + 過去分詞**...**表示過去有能力做，卻沒有做。

例 Glen could have learned Spainish well, but he didn't have time.
格蘭本來可以學好西班牙文，但他沒有時間。

例 I could have sung all night. But my mom asked me to go home.
我本來可以唱一整夜，但我媽要我回家。

表示有能力做某事的片語可用 **be** 動詞 **+ able to**

例 He is able to fix your problems now. = He can fix your problems now.
他現在有能力解決你的問題。

例 I was able to help Teresa the other day.
我前幾天有能力幫助德蕾莎。

例 I could have been able to help Teresa the other day.
我前幾天本來有能力幫助德蕾莎。(但可惜我並沒幫她)

例 I will be able to help Teresa tomorrow.
我明天將有能力幫助德蕾莎。

表示要求或許可的助動詞**...may**

例 You may go home now.
你現在可以回家了

例 You may not leave this classroom.
你不可以離開這個教室。

例 May I borrow your eraser?
我可以借你的橡皮擦嗎？

例 May I have another cup of coffee?
我可以再喝一杯咖啡嗎？

通常要求許可也可用 **Can I**，但 **May I** 較禮貌。

例 Can I use your phone?
我可以用你的手機嗎？

例 Can I ask a question, please?
我可以問一個問題嗎？

could 用在問句也是禮貌的用法，表示請求對方許可。前面提過 **could** 是 **can** 的過去式，但這裡 **could** 用在現在式。

例 Could I have a lift?
可以載我一程嗎？(現在式)

例 Could I have my bill please?
我可以買單嗎？(現在式)

例 Couldn't he come with us?
他不能和我們一起來嗎？(現在式)

might 是 **may** 的過去式，但如果用在問句請求對方許可時，也是禮貌的用法， 與 **could** 相同用在現在式。

例 Might I ask you a question?
我可以問你一個問題嗎？

例 Might I suggest an idea?
我可以提一個建議嗎？

could 也可用在過去許可

例 She could drive her father's car when she was only 15.
當她只有15歲時，就可以開父親的車。

有些讀者可能覺得困惑，為什麼can可表示能力，又可表示許可？ 為什麼could可用在現在式與過去式？這正是英文最複雜的地方，但只要讀者多累積經驗，並從前後文判斷，就可正確了解使用方式。

might與**may**可用在現在式或不久的未來，表示可能性。

例 Jack may not be retired.
傑克可能還沒退休。

例 It might snow.
現在可能會下雪。

例 They might be sweeping the floor now.
現在他們可能正在掃地。

might have + 過去分詞...表示過去可能

例 He might have tried to give me some tips yesterday.
他昨天可能試圖給我一些提示。

例 Sean might not have taken the MRT. He might have walked home.
西恩可能沒坐地鐵。他可能走路回家了。

can 也可表示可能，用在現在式。

例 In Singapore, it can be very hot in summer.
在新加坡，夏天可能很熱。

例 Try this! You can easily lose weight.
嘗試這個！你可以輕鬆減肥。

例 That can't be true.
這不可能是真的。

例 You cannot be serious.
你不可能是認真的。

例 You can't be hungry. You've just eaten.
你不可能會餓，你才剛吃過。

could not 表示過去不可能

例 We knew it could not be him.
我們知道這不可能是他。

例 He was obviously joking. He could not be a pitcher.
他顯然在開玩笑。他不可能是投手。

could have + 過去分詞...表示過去可能性

例 He didn't say hi to me. He could have forgotten my name.
他沒有對我說嗨。他可能忘記我的名字。

例 It's so dangerous! You could have broken your neck yesterday.
太危險了！你昨天可能會摔斷脖子。

might have + 過去分詞...表示過去可能性

例 Harry doesn't show up. He might have got stuck in traffic.
哈利沒出現他，他可能遇上交通堵塞。

例 He might have forgotten that we were meeting today.
他可能忘記了我們今天要開會。

should have + 過去分詞...表示過去可能性

例 She shouldn't have left work yet. I'll call her office.
她應該還沒離開工作。我將打電話去她的辦公室。

Must...應該是…

例 It's getting dark. It must be quite late.
天快黑了。現在應該很晚了

例 You must have heard the good news.
你應該已經聽到好消息。

建議可用 **might, ought to, should**

例 You might visit the botanical gardens.
建議您參觀植物園。

例 You might not want to eat this cake.
你可能不會想吃這個蛋糕。(我不建議你吃)

例 Margaret ought to treat him more tenderly.
瑪格麗特應該更溫柔地對待他。

例 Mark ought not drink so much.
馬克不該喝太多。(注意ought not後面沒加to)

例 You should brush your teeth before you go to bed.
你睡覺前應該刷牙。

Shall 可表示建議 (用在問句)

例 Shall we stay or go out?
我們該留下還是外出？

例 What time shall we meet?
我們該什麼時候見面？

had better 最好 (雖然 **had** 是 **have** 的過去式，但 **had better** 卻是表示現在或未來。)

例 You had better take your umbrella with you.
你最好帶你的傘。

You had better not walk that far.

你最好不要走那麼遠。(had better後面加not)

例 I'd better take it seriously. (I'd better = I had better)
我最好把它當真。

有義務必須做某件事...可用 **must, have to, should, ought to**

例 You must stop at the red light.
你必須停紅燈。

例 You mustn't smoke in the hospital.
你不能在醫院吸煙。(mustn't = must not)

例 I have to send an urgent email.
我必須發一封緊急郵件。

例 You didn't have to score 50 points in that game last night.
你昨晚那場比賽沒有必要得到50分。

例 I'll have to speak to him this coming weekend.
我必須在週末對他說話。

例 I've got to take this book back to the library.
我必須把這本書帶回圖書館。(have got to = have to)

例 I should clean the room once a day.
我應該每天清理一次房間。

例 You ought to take his advice on this issue.
你應該就這個問題接受他的建議。

shall 也可表示有義務做某件事 **(**用於正式文件**)**

例 You shall abide by the law.
你要遵守法律。

例 Congressmen shan't enter this room. (shan't = shall not)
國會議員不得進入這個房間。

should have+ 過去分詞：可表示過去應該要做卻沒做

例 Olivia should have sent everybody a reminder.
奧利維亞應該寄給大家提醒函。(但她沒有)

例 They should have remembered you're a vegetarian. But they served you a meat dish.
他們應該記得你吃素。但他卻為你送上肉。

例 I shouldn't have shouted at you this morning. I apologize.
今天早上我不應該向你大叫。我道歉。

Would 是 **will** 的過去式，表示將要…

例 I thought I'd be late again.
我以為我會再次遲到了。(I would 和I had的簡寫都是I'd，所以要從前後文判斷是哪一個。)

例 I guessed he would only buy the red one the next day. Actually he also bought the green one.
我猜他第二天只會買紅色的。其實他也買了綠色的。

例 In 2014, he promised he would send me a postcard from Peru.
2014年他答應他會從秘魯寄給我一張明信片。

would always 表示過去的老習慣

例 My mother would always make lemon pies in summer.
我母親總是在夏天做檸檬派。

do 強調語氣

例 I do care about you!
我真的在乎你！

例 She did have a lots of fashion magazines!
她確實有很多時尚雜誌！

例 Do visit that place!
一定要參觀那裏！

練習題

請在(a) (b) (c) (d) 中選出正確答案（可能是複選）

1. 何者正確？

(a) He looks happy. (b) He looks at her happy.

(c) He looks happily. (d) He looks at her happily.

2. 何者正確？

(a) I started to watch TV since 7pm. (b) I started to watching TV since 7pm. (c) I started watching TV since 7pm. (d) I started watch TV since 7pm.

3. He had dinner with me before ____.

(a) leave (b) left (c) leaving (d) to leave

4. I want ____ Korean.

(a) learn (b) learning (c) to learn (d) to learning

5. I'll call you while I ____ in Tainan.

(a) am (b) will be (c) being (d) be

6. She ____ like a tiger.

(a) can run (b) can runs (c) cans run (d) cans runs

7. He was ____ you.

(a) able help (b) able to help (c) able to helping (d) able helping

8. We had better ____ our room.

(a) clean (b) cleaning (c) to clean (d) to cleaning

9. We ____ Spanish for 3 years.

 (a) have learned (b) have been learning (c) have learning (d) have been learned

10. I ____ a song.

 (a) am writing (b) am being writing (c) am written (d) am being written

1. (a) (d) look是連綴動詞，後面接形容詞。looks happy----看起來很高興。Look at是一般動詞，後面用副詞happily。
2. (a) (c) start後面可接動名詞或不定詞，兩者意義相同。
3. (c) 介係詞before後面接動名詞。
4. (c) want後面接不定詞。
5. (a) while, when等時間副詞後面句子不可用未來式。
6. (a) 助動詞can本身不加s，後面的動詞也用原形。
7. (b) be動詞 + able to + 原形動詞。
8. (a) had better後面接原形動詞。
9. (a) (b) 現在完成式和現在完成進行式都可以用，後者強調動作正在進行。
10. (a) 主詞 I 在前面，只有現在進行式是對的。

Part 10

7W 問句、附加問句、回應方式

● 7W 問句

7W...what (什麼), which (哪一個), why (為何), who (誰), when (何時), where (何地), how (如何)
be動詞問句型態為：將7W放在句首，be動詞放在7W後面。

例 What is this?
這是什麼？

例 Who are you?
你是誰？

例 When is David leaving?
大衛什麼時候離開？

例 Where are my earrings?
我的耳環在哪裡？

例 Which is her favorite food?
她最喜歡的食物是哪一種？

例 Why were you so happy?
你為什麼這麼開心？

例 How was your trip?
你的旅途如何？

一般動詞問句型態為：將 7W 放在句首， do, have 或其他助動詞放在 7W 後面。

例 What do you want?
你想要什麼？

例 Why did you do that?
你為什麼這麼做？

例 Which do you prefer?
你偏好哪個？

例 Where do you live?
你住在哪裡？

例 How did you make it?
你是怎麼辦到的？

例 When did you see the singer?
你什麼時候看到歌手？

例 Who do you know?
你認識誰？

例 What have you done?
你做了什麼？

例 Who had she met?
她見過誰？

例 Where have you been?
你去哪兒了？

例 When have all the flowers gone?
什麼時候花不見了？

例 Which has he chosen?
他選哪個？

例 Why has the sailor abandoned the ship?
為什麼水手放棄了船？

例 How has the artist earned one billion?
藝術家如何賺取十億？

例 Why can't this be true?
這為什麼不能是真的？

例 Where should I put this box?
我該將這個盒子放在哪裡？

例 How may I help you?
我怎樣能幫到你？

例 When can I see you again?
我何時才能再見到你？

例 What could I say?
我能說什麼？

例 Which would you like?
你喜歡哪個？

例 Who might be interested?
誰可能有興趣？

What kind of...何種的？

Ⓐ What kind of music do you like?
你喜歡什麼樣的音樂？

B I like Jazz.
我喜歡爵士樂。

What time = when...何時？

例 What time did you go shopping?
你什麼時候去購物？

Which 與 **What** 的不同處在於：**Which** 是哪一個？

例 What did you bring to the picnic?
你帶了什麼來野餐？（答案可能百百種：三明治、可樂、帳篷、手電筒…）

例 Which did you bring to the picnic? Fried chicken or hamburger?
你帶了哪個來野餐？炸雞或漢堡？（答案二選一）

例 What color do you want?
你想要什麼顏色？（答案隨你講）

例 Which color do you want? Green? Red? Blue?
你想要哪種顏色？綠或紅或藍？（答案三選一）

例 There are two cars over there. Which one is your car? Honda or Ford?
那裡有兩輛車。哪一台是你的？本田還是福特？

誰**...**可分三種：**who** (主格)**, whose** (所有格)**, whom** (受格)

例 Who will vote for him?
誰投票給他？

例 Who is going to do the laundry?
誰將要洗衣服？

例 Whose idea is this?
這是誰的想法？ (Whose：誰的)

例 Whose golden retriever is barking outside?
誰的黃金獵犬在外面吠叫？ (Whose：誰的)

A Whom did you play with?
你和誰玩？ (Whom當成with的受格)

B I played with my niece.
我和我的侄女一起玩。

A Whom did you report to?
你向誰做報告 (Whom當成to的受格)

B Mr. Lee.
李先生。

注意：當代英文中**Whom**已較少使用，可以用**Who**取代。所以上兩句可改成：**Who did you play with?**以及**Who did you report to?**

When...何時？

A When is the orientation for employees?
什麼時候舉行新員工報到說明會？

B Next Monday.
下週一。

Where...何處？

A Where are you from?
你來自哪裡？

B I'm from Wales.
我來自威爾斯。

Why...為何**?**

例 Why don't you take that chance?
你為什麼不把握這個機會？

Why...表示建議時，動詞前面不加助動詞。

例 Why walk when we can get there by bus?
我們可以乘公共汽車去那裡，為什麼要走路呢？

例 Why not ask him now?
為什麼不現在問他？

注意：上面兩句並非真正在問問題，而是在提供建議。

例 Why worry?
為什麼要擔心？(提供建議，並不要求對方給答案。)

例 Why do you worry?
為什麼你擔心？ (希望對方給答案...擔心的原因是甚麼。)

How...如何？

例 How does this machine work?
這台機器如何運作？

How + 形容詞或副詞**...**問對方有多…

例 How old are you?
你幾歲？

例 How fast can he run?
他能跑多快？

例 How high can he jump?
他能跳多高？

例 How far is your school?
你的學校有多遠？

例 How long did you stay in that villa?
你留在這家酒店多久了？ (long指時間的長)

例 How long are his arms?
他的雙臂多長？ (long指長度)

Ⓐ How often do you go to the gym?
你多久去一次健身房？

Ⓑ Twice a week.
每週兩次。

How many (可數)和 **How much** (不可數)問有多少？

例 How many Facebook friends do you have?
你有多少臉書朋友？

例 How much sugar do you need?
你需要多少糖？

例 How much time do we need to solve this puzzle?
我們需要多少時間來解決這個謎題？(time：時間...不可數名詞)

例 How many times have you been to Boston?
你去過波士頓多少次？ (times：次數...可數名詞)

How come...問理由

例 How come I never saw you before?
為什麼我以前從沒見過你？

下列問題並非希望對方給答案，因為答案很明顯了。

例 Who doesn't like chocolate?
誰不喜歡巧克力？

例 Ice cream in the hot summer days! What's wrong with that?
炎熱的夏日來點冰淇淋！那裡不對呢？

else...其他

例 What else can you expect?
你還能期待什麼別的嗎？

例 Who else will give me a hand?
還有誰會幫我？

例 When else can we get together?
其他什麼時候我們可以聚在一起？

例 Where else could I deposit this check?
我可以在別的什麼地方存這張支票？

例 How else could I quit smoking?
我有別的方法可以戒菸嗎？

附加問句

附加問句並非真正問句，只是加強語氣。通常用在口語而非正式書寫文件中。若前面句子使用肯定句，則附加問句改用否定句，反之亦真。
若句子動詞使用be動詞，附加問句也用be動詞，且時態須一致。

例 He is an excellent student, isn't he?
他是一個優秀的學生，不是嗎？

例 You were late, weren't you?
你遲到了，不是嗎？

例 It is a sunny day, isn't it?
這是晴天，不是嗎？

例 They are searching for a new method, aren't they?
他們正在尋找一種新的方法，不是嗎？

例 Peter isn't an athlete, is he? (✓)
Peter isn't an athlete, isn't he? (✕)
彼得不是運動員，是嗎？(前面否定句，附加問句改用肯定句。)

例 They weren't European, were they? (✓)
They weren't European, are they? (✕)
他們不是歐洲人嗎？對吧？(前面過去式，附加問句也用過去式。)

例 There is a post office here, is there? (✕)
There is a post office here, isn't there? (✓)
這裡有間郵局，不是嗎？（前面肯定句，附加問句改用否定句。）

例 Simon and Doug are absent, aren't Simon and Doug? (✕)
Simon and Doug are absent, aren't they? (✓)
賽門和道格缺席，不是嗎？(Simon and Doug 改用 they)

若句子動詞使用一般動詞，附加問句用 do/don't/does/doesn't/did/didn't，且時態須一致。

例 Rita writes good poems, doesn't she?
麗塔詩寫得好，不是嗎？

例 He likes the new CFO, doesn't he?
他喜歡新的財務長，不是嗎？

例 He mistreated her, didn't he? (✓)（前面肯定句，附加問句改用否定句。）

例 He mistreated her, did he? (✕)
他誤待了她，不是嗎？

例 She doesn't care about those refugees, does she? (✓)
She doesn't care about those refugees, doesn't she? (✕)
她不在乎那些難民，不是嗎？（前面否定句，附加問句改用肯定句。）

例 You didn't pay attention to him, do you? (✕)
You didn't pay attention to him, did you? (✓)
你沒有注意他，不是嗎？ (前面過去式，附加問句也用過去式。)

若句子是完成式，附加問句用have/has/had。 若句子使用助動詞，附加問句使用相同助動詞, 且時態須一致。

例 We have reached our destiny, haven't we?
我們已經達到了我們的目的地，不是嗎？

例 He hasn't received your message, has he?
他還沒有收到你的消息，不是嗎？

例 It hasn't snowed, has it?
還沒有下雪了嗎，不是嗎？

例 You should let him know, shouldn't you?
你應該讓他知道，不是嗎？

例 He can lift her up, can't he?
他可以抬起她，不是嗎？

例 You will be there, won't you?
你會在那裡，不是嗎？

祈使句的附加問句較複雜，參考如下。

例 Keep quiet, won't you ?
保持安靜，好嗎？

例 Let's have a cup of coffee, shall we?
我們一起喝杯咖啡，好嗎？

• 回應對方的種類

副詞 so 回應對方

副詞 **so** 有兩個意思

1. 如此 (太)…

例 The kid is so cute!
這孩子太可愛！

例 You are so nice.
你人真好。

2. 也是...用在回應對方，型態為：So + 動詞 (或助動詞) + 主詞。

Ⓐ I'm so thirsty.
我很口渴。

Ⓑ So am I.
我也是。

Ⓐ Jo is a doctor in Barcelona.
喬是巴塞隆那的醫生。

Ⓑ So is Maggie.
Maggie也是。

Ⓐ I was so happy to see Mrs. Chen.
我很高興看到陳太太。

B So were we.

我們也是。

A Susie can sing well.

蘇西可以唱得很好。

B So can Fanny.

芬妮也可以。

A I love Indian food.

我喜歡印度的食物。

B So do I.

我也是。(前面用一般動詞，後面就用do取代)

注意：在動詞基本觀念章節曾提到：回答時do可取代一般動詞。例如：

A Do you have a car?

B可回答： Yes, I have a car. 或者：Yes, I do. (do取代have a car以避免重複)

A Nina has passed the exam.

尼娜已通過考試。

B So have the other students.

所有其他學生也是。(前面用完成式，後面就用完成式，have對應has。)

副詞 **either** 與 **neither (也不)...**用在回應對方，放在句尾。

neither = not… either。有 **neither** 就不可再用 **not**。

A Jonathan doesn't speak Finnish.

強納森不會說芬蘭語。

B I don't either.

我也不會。(這句也可回答：Neither do I.)

A He isn't ready to go.

他還沒準備好要去。

B We aren't either.

我們也還沒。(這句也可回答：Neither are we.)

A Howard is not a baseball player.

霍華德不是棒球運動員。

B I am not, too. (╳)

我也不是。(too只能用在肯定句，這裡要回答：I am not, either. 或者：Neither am I.)

A Eugene didn't attend to her wedding.

尤金沒有參加她的婚禮。

B I didn't, neither. (╳)

我也沒有。(didn't 已經有not ，所以不能用neither，這裡要回答：I didn't, either. 或者：Neither did I.還有另一種回答方式也可通：Me neither.)

A Mark cannot type 100 words a minute.

馬克無法每分鐘輸入100個字。

B Neither can I. (I can't, either.)

我也不能。

A They haven't lost their dignity.

他們沒有失去尊嚴。

Ⓑ Nor has Brenda.

布蘭達也沒有。(Nor可替換Neither。前面用完成式，後面就用完成式，have對應has。)

Ⓐ Their coworkers won't be joining the parade this year.

他們的同事今年不會參加遊行。

Ⓑ Neither will we.

我們也不會。

例 Sam doesn't play trumpet. He doesn't play French horn, either. = Sam doesn't play trumpet, neither does he play French horn.
山姆不吹小號，他也不吹法國號。

例 He who does not work, neither shall he eat. = He who does not work shall not eat, either.
不工作的人，也不該吃飯。

練習題

請在(a) (b) (c) (d) 中選出正確答案（可能是複選）

1. 何者正確？

   (a) What that is? (b) What is that? (c) That is what?

   (d) Is that what?

2. 何者正確？

   (a) What you need? (b) What do you need?

   (c) Which you need? (d) Which do you need?

3. A: What kind of movies do you like?

   B: ____

   (a) Yes, I like movies. (b) Action movies. (c) I saw a movie yesterday (d) That movie is very good!

4. ____ do you prefer? Milk or Juice?

   (a) What (b) Which (c) Who (d) When

5. ____ car is that?

   (a) Who (b) Whom (c) Whose (d) Why

6. A: ____ don't you come with me?

   B: I don't have time.

   (a) What (b) How (c) Why (d) When

7. A: How ____ did you stay in Taiwan?

   B: 8 weeks.

   (a) far (b) often (c) fast (d) long

8. He is very cute, ____

   (a) isn't he? (b) wasn't he? (c) doesn't he? (d) is he?

9. A: I cannot eat so much food in one day.

   B: ____

   (a) Nor can I (b) I can't, either (c) So can I. (d) I can't, too.

10. ____ may I help you?

    (a) What (b) Which (c) How (d) Why

1. (b) 只有What is that?這種說法，其他全是錯的。
2. (b) (d) 7W問句中，一般動詞前面要用助動詞do, does, did。
3. (b) 題目是問你喜歡哪種電影，所以回答是動作片。
4. (b) 題目是問你喜歡牛奶或果汁，所以是Which。
5. (c) 題目是問誰的貓？用所有格Whose。
6. (c) B的回答是：我沒時間，顯然A是問：你爲何不來？
7. (d) B的回答是8星期，所以A應該是問：你在台灣待多久？問多長時間用how long。
8. (a) 問句是is，因此附加問句要用isn't。前面肯定句，後面就否定句，反之亦然。
9. (a) (b) so can I是附和對方的說法，既然A已經說他不行，B再回答：我也行就不合邏輯。所以 (c) 錯。(d) 錯在too只能用在肯定句。
10. (c) How may I……是英文中常見用法，表示：我可以如何…..？

Part 11

連接字或連接片語

連接詞或連接片語...將一個以上的字或者句子連接起來

Although (though)...雖然

例 Although he is very old, he goes swimming every morning.
雖然他很老，他每天早上都要游泳。(Although放句首)

例 The temperature is still high although it was around mid-night.
= It was around midnight. The temperature is still high
雖然接近午夜，氣溫仍然很高。(although放句中連接兩個句子)

例 Though Brian was the most intelligent student, he didn't get an A.
雖然布萊恩是最聰明的學生，但他沒有得到A。
(although = though)

例 That boss was very demanding, he accepted the job offer though.
那位老闆要求非常高，他還是接受了這份工作。
(though常放在句尾，although不能放句尾)

注意：上面這句**though**是放在後面，意思是「依然」或「還是」，而非「雖然」。**though**放在前面或後面意思不同。

例 His wife disrespected him, He loved her though.
他的妻子不尊重他，他依然愛她。

after all...畢竟

例 She should be able to tell right from wrong. She is 18, after all.
她應該能夠分辨對錯。畢竟她已經18歲。(after all放句尾)

例 I do want to help him. After all, he is my best friend.
我真的想要幫助他，畢竟他是我最好的朋友。(after all放句首)

and 連接字，意思是：和。**and** 連接句子，意思是：而且。

例 Not everyone loves fish and chips in England.
在英國，不是每個人都愛炸魚和薯條。(and連接兩個字)

例 Both Smith and James are very common last names.
史密斯和詹姆斯都是非常常見的姓。(both…and這個片語連接兩個字)

例 The door opened. The man walked in. = The door opened and the man walked in.
門打開了，而且男人走了進去。(and連接兩個句子)

例 I have spoken to the manager, and she has confirmed the delivery date.
我跟經理說過，她已經確認了交貨日期。(and連接兩個句子)

例 The blue line connects E and F, and P and Q. = The blue line connects E and F. The blue line also connects P and Q.
藍線連接E和F，P和Q。(第一和第三個and連接兩個字，第二個and連接兩個句子。)

as ...表示原因

例 As he was late, he is not talking to his advisor now.
因為他遲到了，所以他現在無法跟他的顧問說話。

例 As I was hungry, I decided to grab something to eat.
因為我餓了，我決定抓點東西來吃。

as ...如同

例 Do exactly as I told you.
完全照我說的去做。

例 When in Rome, do as the Romans do.
在羅馬，羅馬人做什麼你就跟著做。(片語：入境隨俗)

as soon as... 同時、立刻

例 I'm going home as soon as you have arrived.
你何時到我就立刻回家。

as long as...只要

例 I am willing to tell you the truth as long as you will keep this secret.
只要你保守這個秘密，我願意告訴你真相。

例 Its legs are as long as this stick.
它的腿與這根棍子一樣長。(這裡的as long as就不是：只要)

but 連接兩個字，表示：但卻是

例 It is a small but practical kitchen.
這是一個小而實用的廚房。

例 They were poor but happy.
他們窮但很快樂。

despite = in spite of... 雖然。後面加名詞或動名詞。

例 He had all the resources. He refused to share with others.
= In spite of all his resources, he refused to share with others.
儘管他有所有的資源，他拒絕與他人分享。

例 Despite the inconvenience, he participated in this project.
儘管不方便，他仍參加了這個計畫。

either···or (兩者之一), **neither···nor** (兩者皆非)**...**兩者皆單數，動詞也用單數。其中有一複數，動詞也用複數。

例 Either Leila or Vincent has to run errands.
萊拉或文森特其中一個必須跑腿。(兩者皆單數，動詞也用單數。)

例 Neither Terence nor Don will get paid.
Terence和Don都不會得到報酬。

例 Either the teacher or the students are to deal with this problem.
老師或學生有一方必須要處理這個問題。(其中有一複數，動詞也用複數。)

例 Max is neither clever nor humorous.
馬克斯既不聰明也不幽默。

例 Max is neither a prentice nor intelligent. (✕)
馬克斯既不是學徒也不聰明。(a prentice是名詞，intelligent是形容詞，兩邊詞性不一違反一致原則。)

注意：neither nor = not either…or。所以，用neither nor就不再加not。

例 I didn't fail neither math nor chemistry. (✕) (用neither nor 就不再加not)

例 I fail neither math nor chemistry. (✓)

例 I didn't fail either math or chemistry. (✓)
我數學和化學都沒被當。

例 Either you get out of my sight or I will call the police.
離開我的視線，否則我會打電話報警。（連接兩個完整的句子）

例 Kimberly could neither laugh nor cry.
金柏莉笑哭不得。(連接兩個動詞）

even if 或 **even though**：即使

例 Even if I have tried to cheer him up, he still looks sad.
即使我試圖逗他開心，他仍然看起來悲傷。

例 Todd can't catch the train even though he has run for minutes.
即使陶德跑了幾分鐘，也趕不上火車。

even so：即使如此

例 Pam was arrogant and rude. Even so, they still hired her.
潘姆傲慢無禮。即使如此，他們仍然僱用她。

in case ：假使，後面接句子。**in case of** 後面接名詞。

例 We have put it down for you in case you didn't understand very well.
我們已經把它寫下來了，以防你不太了解。

例 Use the emergency exit in case of fire.
如有火災，請使用緊急出口。

not only…but also：不只…也是

例 She was not only attractive but also friendly.
她不僅有吸引力，而且友善。(連接兩個形容詞)

例 Richard has eaten not only the steak but also the lamb chop.
理查不僅吃了牛排，還吃了羊排。(連接兩個名詞)

例 He not only lied to us but also spread rumors about us.
他不僅對我們撒謊，還散播關於我們的謠言。(連接兩個句子)

so + 形容詞或副詞 + **that** + 句子：如此…以致於

例 It was so bright that we couldn't open our eyes.
它是如此的明亮，以致於我們睜不開眼睛。

例 These items were so expensive that no one could afford them.
這些物品太貴了，以致於沒有人能負擔得起。

例 He danced so well that they offered him a scholarship.
他舞得如此好，所以他們給了他一個獎學金。

例 My uncle visits us so rarely that my kids can't even recognize him.
我的叔叔很少拜訪我們，所以我的孩子甚至不能認出他。

用 **so that** 連接句子

例 He turned down the music so that he wouldn't disturb others.
他將音樂關小聲，所以他不會打擾別人。

例 He made some money so that he can travel to the Iceland.
他賺了一些錢，所以他可以去冰島旅行。

so as to 或 **in order to** 表示：為了…。**so as not to/in order not to** 表示：為了不要…

例 He cut his hair in order to be praised by his parents.
他剪了頭髮，為了得到父母的稱讚。

例 They moved to downtown so as to take care of their grandma.
他們搬到市中心去為了照顧他們的奶奶。

例 Roger woke up early in order not to be late.
羅傑起得早為了不要遲到。

例 She is on a diet so as not to get fat.
她正在節食為了不要胖。

such + 名詞+ **that** + 句子：如此…以致於

例 He used to be such a liar that no one believes in him now.
他以前是一個如此愛說謊的人以致於現在沒人相信他。

例 Don has such a big yard that I literally got lost.
唐有如此大的院子以致於我真的迷路了。

用 **that** 連接句子 **(that** 後面的句子常稱為子句**)**

例 I think that he is the best player of all time.
我認為他是有史以來最好的球員。

例 Cindy admitted that she had made a mistake.
辛迪承認她犯了一個錯誤。

例 There was a chance that he would find a way out.
他有機會找到出路。

例 The funny thing is that I don't even know her.
有趣的是我甚至不認識她。

例 The police informed everybody (that) it was a false alarm.
警方通知大家這是一場虛驚。(通常that可省略)

例 I am sorry (that) he can't join us.
我很遺憾他不能加入我們。(省略that)

Whenever (無論何時)， wherever (無論何地)， whoever (無論何人)

例 He goes out whenever the weather is fine.
無論何時只要天氣好他都出門。

例 She always laughs whenever he makes that face.
無論何時只要他做那個表情，她總是會笑。

例 I will go with you wherever you want me to.
無論你想要我去哪裡，我都會和你一起去。

例 I will live wherever there's a Chinese restaurant.
我會住在任何有中國餐館的地方。

例 Whoever comes first will get a free drink.
不論是誰第一個到達，將會得到一杯免費飲料。

例 Whoever can solve this riddle will win a round trip ticket to Hawaii.
不論是誰能解決這個謎語，將贏得夏威夷的往返機票。

whether A or B：不論是 A 或 B

例 Whether you order pizza or cook yourself is your decision.
不論您是訂比薩或自己做飯是您自己的決定。(用單數動詞is)

A + rather than + B：寧可 A 不要 B

例 I should google it rather than ask him.
我應該用google搜尋，而不是問他。

例 I decided to drink some milk rather than eat that soup.
我決定喝一些牛奶，而不是喝那湯。(英文中湯用吃的... eat)

7w問題與其他句子結合後，須將疑問句型態改回一般句子型態。

例 What was she doing?
她在做什麼？

例 I wondered what she was doing. (✓)
I wondered what was she doing. (✕)
我納悶她在做什麼。

例 Why is she angry with me?
為什麼她對我生氣？

例 I don't understand why she is angry with me. (✓)
I don't understand why is she angry with me. (✕)
我不明白為什麼她對我生氣。

例 What is it?
它是什麼？

例 Tell me what it is.
告訴我它是什麼。

例 What are you looking for?
你在尋找什麼？

例 A house like that is what you're looking for.
像這樣的房子正是你在尋找的。

例 Why should I stay?
我為什麼要留下？

例 Is there any reason why should I stay? (✕)
Is there any reason why I should stay? (✓)
有什麼理由我應該留下？

例 What you do is more important than what you say.
你所做的比你所說的更重要。

例 What you have done moved me to tears. (✓)
What have you done moved me to tears. (✕)
你所做的讓我感動落淚。

例 Where you go is not my business! (✓)
Where do you go is not my business! (✕)
你去哪裡不干我的事！

7w ＋ to ＋ 動詞

例 The problem is where to raise USD2,000,000.
問題是去哪裡籌集200萬美元。

例 She showed me how to use the vending machine.
她向我展示如何使用自動販賣機。

例 Do you know what to do?
你知道該怎麼辦嗎？

例 Does she know when to press the button?
她知道什麼時候按下按鈕？

例 Please tell me who to ask for help.
請告訴我該向誰要求幫助。

例 Can anyone suggest where to find a convenient store?
有誰可以建議去哪裡找一間便利商店？

例 Ricky hasn't determined which rule to follow.
Ricky沒有決定要遵循哪個規則。

關係代名詞

前面曾談到 7W，它們在文法上的術語是：疑問代名詞。例如：What is this? What是什麼，用來代表不知道的東西。如果對方回答：This is a book. 那麼What就是指book，所以What是代名詞...代替book。又因為對方未回答前無法知道What是什麼，所以稱為：疑問代名詞。

又例如：He didn't know where to go (他不知該去哪。). where是地方的代名詞，又因為不知去哪裡，所以稱為：疑問代名詞。

然而從現在起，Who, which, whose, that等有了新的角色：關係代名詞。

例 The book inspired you. I have read the book.
這本書啟發了你。我讀過這本書。

例 I have read the book which inspired you.
我讀過這本啟發你的書。(which是關係代名詞，表示：the book，用which連接兩個句子。)

例 I bumped into a man. The man's brother is a cop.
我碰到一個男人。這個男人的兄弟是警察。

例 I bumped into a man whose brother is a cop.
我碰到一個男人他的兄弟是警察。(whose是關係代名詞，表示：The man's。)

例 I had an uncle whom I inherited a lot of money from. (✓)
I had an uncle from whom I inherited a lot of money. (✓) (介係詞from可移到whom的前面)
I had an uncle from who I inherited a lot of money. (✓) (現代英文who可取代受格whom)
我有一個叔叔，我從他那裏繼承了很多錢。

例 I need a knife which I can cut this rope with.
I need a knife with which I can cut this rope. (介係詞with可移到which的前面)
我需要一把刀讓我可以用它剪繩子。

例 This is the girl who I bought a flower for.
This is the girl for who I bought a flower. (介係詞for可移到who的前面)
就是這女孩，我買了一朵花給她。

注意：前面看到的都是兩段式結構，也就是關係代名詞連接兩個句子 (A + B)。接下來介紹三段式：關係代名詞的句子放在另一個句子中間 (A1 + B + A2)。

例 You love the woman. The woman is my classmate.
你愛這女人。這女人是我的同學。

如果將這兩句結合起來就變成：The woman who you love is my classmate.

你愛的女人是我的同學。(who是關係代名詞，表示：The woman，用who連接兩個句子。將who you love插在The woman is my classmate. 的中間。)

例 The young lady is a stewardess. You met the young lady yesterday.

那位小姐是個空姐。你昨天遇見了那位小姐。

例 The young lady who you met yesterday is a stewardess.

你昨天遇見的那位小姐是個空姐。(who表示：The young lady，將who you met yesterday插在The young lady is a stewardess.的中間。)

例 The seat is red. The seat is taken.

這座位是紅色的。這座位有人坐了。

例 The seat which is red is taken.

紅色的座位有人坐了。(which是關係代名詞，表示：The seat，將which is red插在The seat is taken.的中間。)

The seat which is red is taken. 和The seat which is taken is red. 這兩句有何不同？

第一句表示：只有一個紅色的座位，而且這個座位被人坐了。

第二句表示：只有一個座位被人坐了，而且這個座位是紅色的。

例 They live in an apartment. The roof of the apartment is colorful.
They live in an apartment whose roof is colorful.
他們住在彩色屋頂的公寓裡。(whose除了指人的，也可指東西的。這裡是指公寓的)

關係代名詞限定性

三段式結構的關係代名詞，到目前為止我們看到都是限定的，也就是說關係代名詞後面的句子對整句的意思有決定性的影響，如果拿掉這個部分可能會讓人搞不清楚。例如：The young lady who you met yesterday is a stewardess. 很多小姐都是空服員，然而這裡專指你昨天遇見的那個，如果不說who you met yesterday，可能讓人不知道是哪一個young lady。

又例如：The woman who you love is my classmate. 我可能有很多女的同學，這裡專指你愛的那個。如果不說who you love，可能讓人不知道是哪一個woman。

例 The apple which is lying on the table is green.
躺在桌子上的蘋果是綠色的。(專指躺在桌子上的那個蘋果，所以which is lying on the table對整句有決定性的影響。)

上面看完限定性的介紹，那非限定性呢？對於整句而言，非限定性的關係代名詞引導的句子可有可無，就算拿掉也不會讓人誤會。

例 My sister who is a nurse always encourages me to eat healthy.
我的護士妹妹總是鼓勵我要吃得健康。
我可能不只一個妹妹，所以要強調是當護士的那個。
這就是限定性。

例 My mother, who is a nurse, always encourages me to eat healthy.
我的母親是護士，她總是鼓勵我要吃得健康。
我只有一個母親，所以就算將who is a nurse拿掉，也不會讓人誤以為我是講別人。這就是非限定性。

注意：上面兩句中可看非限定性who is a nurse前後有加逗點，限定性則沒有，這是文法規則。

例 My history teacher Freddie Simpson, who was a pilot, is a really nice guy.
我的歷史老師弗雷迪辛普森(他曾是飛行員)是一個非常好的人。
這裡已經指名道姓了，不管他以前是不是飛行員，都不影響整個句子的清楚性。
因為這句是非限定性，所以who was a pilot前後有加逗點。

注意：限定性的關係代名詞通常可用that取代，非限定性則不行。

例 It was John who(that) broke the window.
是約翰打破了窗戶。(who可用that替代)

例 It was the window which(that) John broke.
那是被約翰打破的窗戶。(which可用that替代)

例 The car that you desire is not for sale.
你想要的那輛車是不出售的。

注意：限定性的情形下，若關係代名詞前面是受詞，則關係代名詞可省略。但若關係代名詞前面是主詞，則不可省略。

例 The kid who you instructed is a genius. (✓)
The kid you instructed is a genius. (✓)
你教導的那孩子是一個天才。(kid是instruct的受詞，who可省略。)

例 The kid who instructed other kids is a genius. (✓)
The kid instructed other kids is a genius. (✕)
那個指導其他孩子的孩子是一個天才。(The kid是主詞，who不可省略。)

注意：非限定性的情形下，關係代名詞一律不可省略。

例 President Hoover, who died in 1964, was born in Iowa. (✓)
President Hoover, died in 1964, was born in Iowa. (✕)
1964年去世的胡佛總統出生於愛荷華州。

例 The famous writer Sam Gibson, whom everyone respects, is coming next week. (✓)
The famous writer Sam Gibson, everyone respects, is coming next week. (╳)
所有人都尊重的著名作家山姆吉布森將在下周到來。

注意：非限定性的情形下，有時which可指前面的句子，which前面加逗號。

例 He was always late, which made me blacklist him.
他總是遲到，這使我把他加入我的黑名單。(which指：他總是遲到這件事)

例 We've lost our map, which means we have to buy a new one.
我們的地圖掉了，這意味著我們必須購買一張新的。(which指：我們的地圖掉了這件事)

例 We've lost our map which was borrowed from a friend.
我們的地圖掉了，那是從朋友借來的。(不加逗號表示限定性，which指地圖)

如前面章節所提，why, when, where可能是副詞。但它們也是關係代名詞。然而初學者不必注意這些細節，只要照下列例句學習如何用來連接句子。

例 This is why she looks so excited.
這就是為什麼她看起來很興奮。

例 Do you know the main reason why she hates me?
你知道她討厭我的主要原因嗎？

例 The restaurant where I usually have dinner is opened till 9PM.
我通常吃晚飯的餐廳開放至晚上9點。

例 Let's go to a place where the sun always shines.
讓我們去一個太陽總是照耀的地方。

例 There are times when I feel like having a Jasmine tea.
有時候我想來杯茉莉花茶。

例 He remembers the days when there were no cell phones.
他記得沒有手機的日子。

關係代名詞前面也可加數量詞

例 A lot of people are present, many of whom I have never seen.
很多人出席，其中很多人我從未見過。

例 He picked up a handful of pebbles, one of which was purple.
他拿起一把鵝卵石，其中一塊是紫色的。

例 She has five brothers, two of whom are attorneys.
她有五個兄弟，其中兩個是律師。

用現在分詞將句子連接

Finding the hoax, the teacher became angry.
發現騙局，老師生氣了。

例 Learning as much as possible, she finally got the degree.
盡可能學習，她終於獲得了學位。

例 Hearing a noise, the burglar ran away.
聽到聲音，小偷跑了。

用過去分詞將句子連接

例 Terrified, Winston called 911. = Winston was terrified, Winston called 911.
嚇到了，溫斯頓叫911。

例 Intrigued, she decided to find out why. = She was intrigued, she decided to find out why.
被勾起興趣後，她決定找出原因。

注意：下面第一句用過去分詞，表示被動：他被欺騙。第二句用現在分詞，表示主動：他欺騙人。

例 Deceived by his own friends, he lost all the money.
被自己的朋友欺騙，他失去了所有的錢。

例 Deceiving his own friends, he got all the money.
欺騙自己的朋友，他得到了所有的錢。

請在(a) (b) (c) (d) 中選出正確答案（可能是複選）

1. It was insulting, he accepted it ____.

   (a) although (b) though (c) however (d) even

2. Can you give me a reason ____ I should help you?

   (a) when (b) how (c) what (d) why

3. He chose a few books, ____ is for his son.

   (a) which (b) one which (c) one of which (d) which one

4. I don't know ____ .

   (a) how angry she was (b) how angry was she (c) how she was angry (d) was she angry

5. ____ your failure, I still love you.

   (a) Despite (b) In spite of (c) Even though (d) As

6. He is neither stupid ____ lazy.

   (a) or (b) nor (c) and (d) also

7. She is ____ that she can't find a boyfriend.

   (a) so tall (b) so at all girl (c) such tall girl (d) such a tall girl

8. Take an umbrella ____.

   (a) in case rain (b) in case of rain (c) in case it rains (d) in case rains

9. Tim was very hard-working. ____, they still fired him.

   (a) Even though (b) Even so (c) Even if (d) As long as

10. ____ I was so thirsty, I bought three bottles of Milk.

    (a) Though (b) Because (c) As (d) Despite

1. (b) though可放在句尾，although和however不能放在句尾，even不合邏輯。
2. (d) 前面用reason，後面接why。
3. (c) 只有one of which是正確用法。
4. (a) 7W的句子如果插在其他句子中間，則主詞放在動詞前面。
5. (a) (b) despite和In spite of後面都可接名詞，Even though後面要接句子而非名詞，用as完全邏輯不通。
6. (b) neither後面接nor。
7. (a) (d) such a tall girl 和so tall才是正確用法。
8. (b) (c) in case of 後面接名詞，in case後面接句子。
9. (b) even so是：即使如此。用此片語整句才合乎邏輯。
10. (b) (c) Because和As都可表示原因。

Part 12

假設語氣與條件式

If only或者wish用在表示不可能為真的假設情況。現在式時，將動詞改為過去式，be動詞用were。過去式時，將動詞改為過去完成式。

例 If only I were a bird.
要是我是一隻鳥就好了。(很明顯我現在不可能是一隻鳥。雖然I的過去式原本是was，但這裡用were。)

例 If only I could find a way.
要是我能找到辦法就好了。(很可惜我現在就是沒辦法)

例 If only I knew how much he loves me.
要是我能知道他有多麼愛我就好了。(可惜他的愛莫測高深，我永遠無法知道。)

例 He wish he were a billionaire!
他希望他是一個億萬富翁！ (可惜他現在不是)

例 I wish she were my wife.
我希望她是我的妻子。(可惜這不可能發生)

例 I wish you wouldn't arrive so late all the time.
我希望你不會始終都遲到。(很遺憾他就是每次遲到)

例 If only I had been more cautious yesterday.
要是我昨天更加謹慎就好。(很遺憾昨天的事已無法改變。這是過去的事，將動詞由過去式改為過去完成式。)

例 If only I had woken up early this morning.
要是我今早早點醒來就好。(很遺憾我今早睡過頭，這已無法改變。這是過去的事，將動詞改為過去完成式。)

例 Rosa wishes she hadn't devoured the cream pies last night.
羅莎希望她昨晚沒有狂吃奶油派。

條件式型態：條件子句 ＋ 逗點＋主要子句 。或者：主要子句＋條件子句。

所謂條件子句前面由 **if** 或 **when** 或 **unless** 帶領。
第 **0** 型：現在或未來確定的情形**...**條件子句、主要子句都用原本時態

例 If you heat ice, it melts.（條件子句在前，主要子句前加逗點）
Ice melts if you heat it. （主要子句在前，不加逗點）
如果你加熱冰，它會融化。(永遠為真的物理現象)
When you heat ice, it melts.（將if改為when，意思完全一樣。）

例 If you visit Taiwan, stay for several days at Kenting.
如果你訪問台灣，在墾丁待幾天。(建議不隨情況改變)

例 If you've done that, go and have a break.
如果你做完，去休息一下。(只要你做完就可休息)

例 When I'm listening to music, please don't make any noise.
當我聽音樂時，請不要發出任何噪音。

第 **1** 型：現在或未來不確定會不會發生的情形...條件子句用原本時態、主要子句用未來式或加助動詞。

例 If we give John a ride, he'll be really pleased.
如果我們載約翰一程，他會很高興。(不確定我們會不會載他)

例 Unless we hurry, we won't be in time for the movie.
除非我們快點，否則我們無法及時趕上電影。(不確定我們有沒有辦法快點)

例 If Isaiah is feeling better, he'll tell us.
如果以賽亞感覺好一點，他會告訴我們的。(不確定他好了沒)

例 If you haven't told Phil about it, I'll tell him.
如果你還沒告訴菲爾，我會告訴他的。(不確定你說了沒)

例 I might show you my collection if you drop by.
我可能讓你看我的收藏，如果你來訪。(不確定你會不會來，show前面加might表示可能)

例 We should cross out the mistakes in case he doesn't understand.
我們應該刪除錯誤以防他不明白。(不確定他會不會懂，if用in case取代。cross out前面加should表示應該這麼做...當然也可選擇不要這麼做。)

例 Should it rain, there will be no picnic today.
如果下雨，今天不會野餐。(Should放在句首也可表示：如果，用來取代if。)

第 **2** 型：幾乎確定不會發生的情形**...**雖然是現在或未來，但條件子句用過去式 **(be** 動詞用 **were)**，主要子句用 **would** + 動詞。

例 If I had time, I would celebrate with you.
如果我有時間，我會和你一起慶祝。(抱歉這不可能發生，因為現在真的沒時間。)

例 If I were elected president next year, I would build a new subway line.
如果我明年當選總統，我會建一條新的地鐵線。(我明年不可能當選總統)

例 If the sun was shining, I would go to the beach.
如果太陽照耀著，我會去海灘。(很遺憾現在陰天)

例 I would propose to her if I were you. (✓)
I would propose to her when I were you. (✕)
如果我是你，我會向她求婚。(因為不可能發生，所以不能用when。)

例 If he was able to jump that high, he would be a basketball player now.
如果他能夠跳那麼高，他現在是籃球員。

例 Unless he had permission from his parents, he wouldn't go out for a beer.
除非得到父母的許可，否則他不能出去喝啤酒。(他父母不可能許可)

例 He could get a new job if he really tried.
如果他真的嘗試，他可以得到新的工作。(問題他不嘗試)

例 If I lived in 20th century, I'd buy a camera.
如果我住在 20 世紀，我會買一台相機。(不可能時光倒流)

注意：下面兩句說明第1型和第2型的差別

例 If I get promoted, I will buy everyone a bubble tea. (第1型...我認為有可能得到晉升)

例 If I got promoted, I would buy everyone a bubble tea. (第2型...我認為得到晉升是不可能的)
如果我得到晉升，我將會請每人一杯珍珠奶茶。

第 **3** 型之 **A**：條件子句和主要子句都是過去已經發生不可能改變的情形，條件子句用過去完成式，主要子句用 **would** 或 **could** 或 **might** + 過去完成式。

例 If I had owned a plane in 2014, I would have flown to New Zealand.
如果 2014 年我有一架飛機，我會飛往紐西蘭。(我沒飛機也沒飛往紐西蘭，兩者都已發生不能改變，所以都用過去完成式。)

例 If I had gone to Seoul, I could have learned Korean.
如果我以前去了首爾，我可能已經開始學韓文。(我沒去首爾也沒開始學韓文，兩者都已發生不能改變，所以都用過去完成式。)

例 If I had had more time, I might have gone to the party.
如果我有更多的時間，我可能會去參加派對。(had had more time...第二個had是have的過去分詞)
(我沒更多時間也沒參加派對。)

注意：其實前面討論助動詞時就已提到**would**或**could**或**might** + 完成式可表示過去沒發生的假設情況，這裡的觀念完全一樣。

例 Unless you had phoned him, he couldn't have known the truth.
除非你已經打電話給他，否則他不會已經了解真相。
(事實是你沒打電話給他，他也不了解真相。)

例 If Melody had been crossing the street, the car would have hit him.
如果美樂蒂當時正在過馬路，那車子可能會撞到她的。(條件子句也可用過去完成進行式，強調：當時正在。) (事實是美樂蒂當時沒有過馬路，也沒被撞。)

注意：如果條件子句的過去完成式前面加**were to**，那表示情況是極端不可能發生或難以想像的。

例 If the fire were to have broken out, it would have caused unthinkable damages.
如果當時火災發生，會造成無法想像的損失。(還好當時沒發生，也沒造成損失。)

例 If Lisa were to have failed the test in June, she would have lost her scholarship.
如果麗莎六月未通過考試，她將已經失去獎學金。(麗莎是優秀的學生，難以想像她會考不過。事實是她既考過也拿獎學金。)

第 3 型之B：條件子句是過去已經發生不可能改變的情形，用過去完成式。主要子句現在的部分用would或could或might ＋ 現在式，未來的部分用would或could或might ＋ 現在式 (或進行式)。

例 I would be a billionaire if I had listened to his advice.
如果當初我聽了他的意見，我現在是一個億萬富翁。(第3型之B)

例 I would have been a billionaire if I had listened to his advice.
如果當初我聽了他的意見，我現在已經是一個億萬富翁。(第3型之A)

注意：其實上面兩句意思差不多。

例 If you had spent all your salary, you wouldn't buy this sweater.
如果你已經花光所有的薪水，你現在不會買這件毛衣。(你沒花光所有的薪水所以你現在正在買這件毛衣。) (第3型之B)

例 If you had spent all your salary, you wouldn't have bought this sweater.
如果你已經花光所有的薪水，你現在不會已經買了這件毛衣。(你沒花光所有的薪水所以你已經買了這件毛衣。) (第3型之A)

例 If you had complained to him like that two days ago, you might be in trouble.
如果你兩天前那樣向他抱怨，你現在可能惹上麻煩。(第3型之B)

例 If Mae had gotten the invitation, she would be moving to Denmark.
如果Mae已經得到邀請，她將正準備搬到丹麥。(第3型之B)

例 If Debby hadn't wasted her savings gambling, she would go to Europe with us next week.
如果Debby沒有將她的儲蓄浪費在賭博，她將在下週與我們一起去歐洲。(第3型之B)

第 **3** 型之 **C**：主要子句是過去已經發生不可能改變的情形，用過去完成式。條件子句是未來的情況用 **were** + 現在分詞。

例 If I weren't going to make a presentation, I would have walked your dog.
如果我不是將要做報告，我已經幫你遛狗。

例 If my parents weren't coming this weekend, I wouldn't have cleaned my room.
如果我的父母本週末不來，我不會已經清理我的房間。

例 If the CIO weren't leaving, I would have asked him to purchase some new routers.
如果資訊長沒要離開，我已經請他購買一些新的路由器。

CEO(chief executive officer)----執行長
COO(chief operating officer)----營運長
CIO(chief information officer)----資訊長
CFO(chief financial officer)----財務長

練習題

請在(a) (b) (c) (d) 中選出正確答案（可能是複選）

1. If only I ____ Bill Gates!

   (a) am (b) will be (c) were (d) have been

2. Glen wishes he ____ so much yesterday.

   (a) didn't drink (b) hadn't drunk (c) drank (d) wouldn't drink

3. ____ we help him, he won't be able to do it.

   (a) If (b) Unless (c) If only (d) When

4. ____, the playground will be closed.

   (a) If it rains (b) If it rain (c) Should it rain (d) Should it rains

5. If I had bought a ticket last week, I ____ LA.

   (a) had visited (b) would visit (c) would have visited (d) have visited

6. 何者正確？

   (a) He will be unhappy if you leave. (b) He will be unhappy, if you leave. (c) If you leave he will be unhappy. (d) If you leave, he will be unhappy.

7. ____ you come to Tainan, be sure to taste the local food.

   (a) If (b) Unless (c) If only (d) When

8. If I had taken his advice, I ____ a professor.
   (a) have become (b) had become (c) would become
   (d) would have become
9. If I win the prize, I ____ you a new car.
   (a) will buy (b) would buy (c) would have bought
   (d) will have bought
10. If Sara ____ you the map, I will show you.
   (a) hasn't shown (b) hadn't shown (c) doesn't show
   (d) couldn't have shown

1. (c) 現在式假設語氣用were，過去式假設語氣用had been。
2. (b) yesterday是過去式，假設語氣用had drunk----過去完成式。
3. (b) 用unless（除非），整句邏輯才通順。
4. (a) (c) if和should放句首都可以當假設語氣（如果），但第三人稱單數時，if後面動詞加s，should後面動詞用原形。
5. (b) (c) 條件子句用過去完成式，表示是與過去事實相反的假設語氣，所以主要子句用would, should, could等助動詞＋have＋過去分詞。另外(b)也可以，請參考第3型之B。

6. (a) (d) 條件子句放前面時，要加逗號。條件子句放後面時，不加逗號。
7. (a) (d) 假設的條件可能爲真（你可能來台灣），可用when代替if。
8. (c) (d) 條件子句用過去完成式，表示是與過去事實相反的假設語氣，所以主要子句用would, should, could等助動詞＋have＋過去分詞。(c) 也對，請參考第 3 型之B。
9. (a) 前面win用現在式，表示假設的情形可能爲真，所以主要子句用未來式。
10. (a) (c) 主要子句用未來式，表示假設的情形可能爲真，條件子句用原本型態，也就是說現在式或現在完成式皆可。

Part 13

標點符號

逗號、句號、驚嘆號、問號、冒號、分號都放在句子最後，與前一個字中間不須空格。但與下一個字中間要空一格。

例 I am a foreigner. I came from Canada. (✓)
I am a foreigner . I came from Canada. (╳)(句號與前一個字foreigner中間不須空格)
I am a foreigner.I came from Canada. (╳)(句號與下一個字I中間須空一格)
我是一個外國人。我來自加拿大。

例 As a matter of fact, I have no idea. (✓)
As a matter of fact,I have no idea. (╳)(逗號與下一個字I中間須空一格)
事實上，我不知道。

例 What a surprise ! The puzzle is solved. (╳)(驚嘆號與前一個字surprise中間不須空格)
太驚奇! 難題解決了。

例 Will he tell us why ? No one knows. (╳)(問號與前一個字why中間不須空格)
他會告訴我們為什麼嗎？沒人知道。

例 He bought two pets:a puppy and a parrot. (╳)(冒號與下一個字a中間須空一格)
他買了兩隻寵物：一隻小狗和一隻鸚鵡。

例 I'm looking forward to seeing you soon;I believe it will be a wonderful experience. (╳)(分號與前一個字soon

中間不須空格，但與I中間須空一格。)
我很期待很快見到你，我相信這將是一個美好的經驗。

連字號：前後都不需空格

例 up-to-date(最新的)
fifty-one(51)
one-third(1/3)

連字號所連結的字不用複數

例 France has a 35-hour work week.(✓)
France has a 35-hours work week. (✕)
法國工時為每週35小時。(hour後面不加s)

例 He is only a five-year-old kid. (✓)
He is only a five-years-old kid. (✕)
他只是一個五歲的孩子。

例 Phil won the 100-metre sprint. (✓)
Phil won the 100-metres sprint. (✕)
菲爾贏得了100米賽跑。

三個句點有暫停的效果，也可表示省略的字。

例 She visits her aunt once a year...whether she likes it or not. (暫停)
她每年都會拜訪阿姨，不管她喜歡還是不喜歡。

例 I don't wanna talk to her. She is very...you know what I mean.(省略)
我不想和她說話。她非常...你知道我的意思。

破折號：冒號、分號、三個句點都可用破折號取代

例 He blamed his divorce on one thing: beer.(✓)

He blamed his divorce on one thing – beer.(✓)

他把他的離婚歸咎於一件事:啤酒

例 Nothing was wrong; the only inconvenience was the location.(✓)

Nothing was wrong – the only inconvenience was the location.(✓)

沒有哪裡不好，唯一的不方便是地理位置。

例 I met no one but...the magician.(✓)

I met no one but – the magician.(✓)

除了魔術師我誰都沒有遇到。

引號用來一字不漏地引述別人的話。
引號與裡面的字之間不用空格，但與引號前後的字要有空格。

例 Her mom said: "Sit down please." (✓)

Her mom said, "Sit down please." (✓)(said後面可用冒號或逗號)

Her mom said: " Sit down please. " (✕)(引號與裡面的字之間不用空格)

Her mom said:"Sit down please." (✕)(引號與前後的字要有空格)

"Sit down please," her mom said. (✓)(引述的內容可放在前面)

她媽媽說：「請坐。」

請注意上面範例。當引述的話放在前面時。最後一個字接逗號而非句號。

當引述的話放在後面時。前面也是接逗號而非句號。

這是因為一個句子裡只能有一個句號。

除了用「說」以外也可用回答(reply)、問(ask)、報告(report)、寫(write)等等。

例 "I wasn't home," he replied.
He replied, "I wasn't home."
He replied: "I wasn't home."
他回答說：「我不在家。」

例 "No one was missing," he reported.
He reported, "No one was missing."
He reported: "No one was missing."
他報導：「沒有人失踪。」

例 Daniel insisted, "Let's go Dutch."
"Let's go Dutch," Daniel insisted.
丹尼爾堅持說：「我們各付各。」

例 Fiona wrote, "Justice finally prevails."
"Justice finally prevails," Fiona wrote.
菲奧娜寫道：「正義終於伸張了。」

但如果前面引述句本身已有問號或驚嘆號，則就不用逗號。

例 "Who gave you this?" the teacher asked. (✓)
"Who gave you this?," the teacher asked. (✕)(已有問號就不用逗號)
"Who gave you this?" asked the teacher.(倒裝句，將 the teacher asked 改成asked the teacher)(✓)
老師問：「誰給你這個？」

例 "I don't understand!" shouted Nathan.
Nathan shouted, "I don't understand!"
納森喊道：「我不明白！」

引述完整句子第一個字大寫

例 Ivy said, "We are more courageous and cooperative, so we will win."
艾薇說：「我們更勇敢更合作，所以我們會贏。」

但若只是引用幾個字則不用大寫

例 Ivy said that they were more "courageous and cooperative," so they will win.
艾薇說她們「更勇敢更合作」，所以她們會贏。

引用字本身不構成斷句，則不用逗號。

例 Somebody invented this word "Linsanity" in 2012.
2012年有人發明了「林來瘋(Linsanity)」這個字。
若引述句是放在句中，則不用逗號。

例 Is "I don't care" all you can say to me?
你只能對我說「我不在乎」嗎？

句號與逗號永遠在引號裡面。

例 The policeman said, "Go straight," then he said, "Turn left."(✓)
The policeman said, "Go straight", then he said, "Turn left". (✕)(句號與逗號在引號外面)
警察說：「直走」，然後他說：「左轉」。

若引述中還有引述，則用單引號。

例 Math teacher said, "In your classroom, I saw 'STUDY HARD!' written on a wall."
數學老師說：「在你的教室裡，我看到牆上寫著:『用功讀書！』。」

直接引述 vs. 間接引述

前面提到引號用來一字不漏地引述別人的話。這稱為直接引述。但英文中還有間接引述，此時就不需要引號。

例 Selina says, "I like bread and butter." = Selina says that she likes bread and butter.
Selina說她喜歡麵包抹奶油。

但間接引述較複雜的是----如果時態不是現在式，就可能需要改變時態。

例 "I always drink coffee", she said. = She said that she always drank coffee.(現在式改成過去式)
她說她向來喝咖啡。

例 She said, "I am tired." = She said that she was tired.
她說她累了。

例 Tommy said, "I am reading a book." = Tommy said that he was reading a book. (現在進行式改成過去進行式)
湯米說他正在讀一本書。

例 She said, "I'll be using the car next Friday". = She said that she would be using the car next Friday.
她說她下週五會使用這輛車。

例 "My family arrived on Saturday," he said. = He said that his family had arrived on Saturday.
他說他的家人星期六抵達。(第九章曾提到比過去更早的時態要用過去完成式，因此arrived改成had arrived。)

例 "I have been to Spain," he told me. = He told me that he had been to Spain.
他告訴我他去過西班牙。

例 He said, "I have been playing football for two hours." = He said that he had been playing football for two hours.
他說他已經踢足球兩個小時。(現在完成進行式改成過去完成進行式)

但如果現在依然為真，則不必改成過去式。

例 "My name is Lynne," she said. = She said her name was Lynne. = She said her name is Lynne.
她說她的名字叫林恩。(過去和現在名字都叫林恩，所以用was或is都可以。)

過去時間表達未來---如果該未來時間已經過了，則 **will** 改成 **would**。

例 "I'll be back by lunchtime," he said. = He said that he would be back by lunchtime.
他說他會在午餐時間回來。(從現在來看，該午餐時間已成過去。)

過去時間表達未來---但如果該未來時間還沒到，則仍然用 **will**。

例 "I'll be back by 2020," he said. = He said that he will be back by 2020.
他說他2020年前會回來。

表示可能、應該的助動詞(might, could, would, should, ought to)不需改變時態

例 Edward explained, "It could be difficult to locate the lost ship." = Edward explained that it could be difficult to locate the lost ship.
愛德華解釋說失蹤的船可能很難被找到。

例 Rose said, "I might bring a bottle of wine to the party." = Rose said that she might bring a bottle of wine to the party.
羅絲說她可能會帶一瓶酒參加派對。

直接引述改成間接引述時，有時須注意改變時間地點用語。

例 "I saw him today," she said. = She said that she had seen him that day.
她說：「我今天看到他。」= 她說她當天見過他。
（由於時間已過，所以不能再用today，要改用that day。）

例 "I saw him yesterday," she said. = She said that she had seen him the day before.
她說：「我昨天看到他。」= 她說她前一天見過他。
（由於時間已過，不能再用yesterday，要改用the day before。）

例 "I met her the day before yesterday," he said. = He said that he had met her two days before.
他說：「我前天看到她。」= 他說他兩天前見過她。
（the day before yesterday改成two days before。）

例 "I'll see you tomorrow," he said.= He said that he would see me the next day.
他說：「明天我會見你的。」= 他說他第二天會見我。
（tomorrow改成the next day或the following day。）

例 "We'll visit here the day after tomorrow," they said. = They said that they would visit here two days later.
他們說：「我們後天再來這裡。」= 他們說他們兩天後會來。（the day after tomorrow改成two days later）

例 "I have an interview next week," she said. = She said that she had an interview the following week.
她說：「我下週有面談。」=她說她下一週有面談。

注意：**next week是下週（從現在開始算），the following week是次一週（從當時開始算），所以過去式時要將next week改成the following week。同理，next month改成the following month。 next year改成the following year。**

例 "Darren went on vacation last week," he told us. = He told us that Darren had gone on vacation the previous week.
他告訴我們，達倫上個星期去休假。= 他告訴我們，達倫前個星期去休假。

注意：last week是上週（從現在開始算），the previous week是前一週（從當時開始算），所以過去式時要將last week改成the previous week。同理，last month改成the previous month。last year改成the previous year。

例 "I sent Irene an email a week ago," he said. = He said he sent Irene an email a week before.
他說：「我一週前就給艾琳發了一封電子郵件。」= 他說他一週前就給了艾琳一封電子郵件。

注意：ago（從現在開始算）和 before（從當時開始算）在英文中意義不同。

例 "I'm getting a new car this week," she said. = She said she was getting a new car that week.
她說：「我本週要有輛新車了。」= 她說她那週將要有輛新車。（將this改成that）

例 "Have you seen the house here?" he asked. = He asked if I had seen the house there.
他問：「你見過這裡的房子嗎？」= 他問我是否看過那裡的房子。（將here改成there）

直接引述改成間接引述時，有時須注意改變人稱

例 Fred said: "I'm going to my friend's house." = Fred said that he was going to his friend's house.
弗雷德說：「我要去我朋友的家。」= 弗雷德說他要去他朋友的家。（將my改成his）

YES / NO 問題，有時直接引述較間接引述更為簡化。

例 "Can I have some milk?" she asked. = She asked for some milk.
她問：「我可以喝一些牛奶嗎？」

例 He asked, "May I have the bill, please?" = He asked for the bill.
他要求買單。

下列情形也可改成if 或 whether的子句

例 He asked, "Do you speak Mandarin?" = He asked me if I spoke Mandarin.
他問我是否說國話。

例 He asked, "Is it snowing?" = He asked if it was snowing.
他問是否下雪了。

例 He asked, "Did you really come by MRT?" = He doubted whether I had come by MRT.
他懷疑我是否坐捷運來的。

平行

英文中的平行是指要注意詞性一致

例 Leon likes playing the flute, the trumpet and play the guitar. (×)
里昂喜歡演奏長笛，小號，吉他。（playing是動名詞，後面再用play就詞性不一致。）
Leon likes playing the flute, the trumpet and the guitar. (✓)
（長笛，小號，吉他都是名詞，詞性一致。）

例 She played basketball, had a shower and gone to school. (×)
她打籃球，洗澡去上學。（played和 had都是過去式，但 gone是過去分詞，前後詞性不一致。）
She played basketball, had a shower and went to school. (✓)

例 She is crazy about watching TV more than to read a book .(×)
她著迷於看電影勝於讀書。（前面用動名詞，後面卻用不定詞，產生不一致。）
She is crazy about watching TV more than reading a book.(✓)

例 Her father wants her not only to clean the kitchen but also doing the laundry.(X)
她的父親希望她不僅要清洗廚房，還要洗衣服。（前面用不定詞，後面卻用動名詞，產生不一致。）
Her father wants her not only to clean the kitchen but also to do the laundry.(✓)

請在(a) (b) (c) (d) 中選出正確答案（可能是複選）

1. 何者正確？

   (a) She's a teacher. She teaches Chemistry. (b) She's a teacher, She teaches Chemistry. (c) She's a teacher. she teaches Chemistry. (d) She's a teacher she teaches Chemistry.

2. Kenny says, “I like grape juice.” =

   (a) Kenny says I like grape juice. (b) Kenny says he likes grape juice. (c) Kenny says like grape juice.
   (d) Kenny says that he likes grape juice.

3. Tony said, “I'm riding my bike.” =

   (a) Tony said he is riding his bike. (b) Tony said he was riding his bike. (c) Tony said he rides his bike.
   (d) Tony said he rode his bike.

4. Joy said, “I'll be there.” =

   (a) Joy said she would beenthere. (b) Joy said she would be there. (c) Joy said she is there (d) Joy said she was there.

5. He said, “You're good!” =

   (a) He said: “You're good!” (b) “You're good!” he said.
   (c) “You're good!” he said: (d) “You're good!,” he said.

6. 何者正確？

   (a) He is a six-year-old kid. (b) He is six years old.

(c) He is a six-years-old kid. (d) He is six year old.

7. 何者正確？

(a) He said, “Move forward” . (b) “Move forward.” He said. (c) “Move forward,” He said. (d) He said, “Move forward.”

8. 何者正確？

(a) She says, “Terry said that's the “motto” we need.”

(b) She says, “Terry said that's the ‘motto' we need.”

(c) She says, ‘Terry said that's the ‘motto' we need.'

(d) She says, ‘Terry said that's the “motto” we need.'

9. Yesterday he told me, “I watered my garden today.” =

(a) Yesterday he told me he watered his garden today.

(b) Yesterday he told me he had watered his garden today.

(c) Yesterday he told me he had watered his garden that day.

(d) Yesterday he told me he has watered his garden that day.

10. 何者正確？

(a) Sandy dislikes her teacher and do homework.

(b) Sandy dislikes her teacher and does homework.

(c) Sandy dislikes her teacher and homework.

(d) Sandy dislikes her teacher and doing homework.

1. (a) (b) 錯在逗點後She的S要改成小寫。(c) 錯在句點後she的s要改成大寫。(d) 錯在同一個句子不可有兩個動詞，中間要用句號或逗號斷開。
2. (b) (d) say後面子句可用that帶領。
3. (b) 前面是Tony said表示過去式，所以後面用過去進行式。
4. (b) 前面是Joy said表示過去式，所以後面要將will改成would。
5. (a) (b) (c) 錯在said放後面時不可用冒號。(d) 錯在引號內有了驚嘆號就不再加逗號。
6. (a) (b) 被連接的字不需用複數。
7. (c) (d) (a) 錯在Move forward後面的句號放在引號外面。(b) 錯在引用句放前面時後面要接逗號而非句號，因爲一個句子裡面只能有一句號。
8. (b) 引用中的引用用單引號。原本的引用仍用雙引號。
9. (c) (b) 錯在間接引述時today要改成that day。(d) 錯在比過去更早的時間要用過去完成式，也就是將has watered改成had watered。
10. (c) (d) her teacher是名詞，爲了符合文法上的平行and後面也要用名詞。Homework和doing homework都算名詞。

Part 14

常見動詞片語與成語

動詞片語 (注意:sb = somebody: 某人 sg = something: 某事)	意義	例句
abide by	遵守	Those soldiers always abide by the law. 這些士兵總是遵守法律。
account for	解釋	Nobody can account for all the misbehaviors. 沒有人可以解釋所有的不當行為。
ask sb out	約某人外出	Brian asked Judy out to dinner. 布萊恩約朱迪去吃飯。
ask over	邀請	Ian asked me over for dinner tonight. 伊恩邀我今晚晚餐。
ask around	四處詢問	I asked around but nobody knew where it was. 我四處問過，但沒有人知道它在哪裡。
back down	退縮	No matter what they say, I won't back down. 不管他們說什麼，我不會退縮。
back off	退開	Back off! Take your hands off me! 退開！把你的手拿開！
back sb up	支持某人	The labor union backed him up over this issue. 工會在這個問題上支持他。
back up	備份資料	You should always back up important files in your computer. 您應該始終備份計算機中的重要文件。

bail out	拯救	How many times does the government have to bail out this bank? 政府要救這家銀行多少次？
be after	追	The police are after the thief. 警察在追小偷。
be cut out for	適合	Ronnie was not cut out for this job. 羅尼不適合這份工作。
be fed up	受夠了	I am fed up with his complaints. 我受夠了他的抱怨。
be into	喜歡	I am not into Jazz music. 我不喜歡爵士樂。
blow up	爆炸	The racing car blew up after it crashed into the wall. 賽車在撞牆後爆炸。
sg break down	故障	His car broke down on highway. 他的車在高速公路上拋錨了。
sb break down	崩潰	Tammy broke down when she heard this tragedy. 當她聽到這個悲劇時，Tammy 崩潰了。
break in	闖入	Two burglars broke in last night and stole all the money. 昨晚有兩個竊賊闖入，偷了所有的錢。
break up	分手	My boyfriend and I broke up. 我的男朋友和我分手了。
bring about	產生	This invention brings about lots of new business chances. 本發明帶來了許多新的商業機會。
bring sb down	讓某人難過	Her sarcasm has brought me down. 她的諷刺使我難過。

bring sb up	撫養長大	His grandparents brought him up. 他的祖父母把他撫養長大。
bump into	巧遇	Wendy bumped into Helen the other day. 溫蒂前幾天巧遇海倫。
call around	四處打電話詢問	We called around but we weren't able to find any house keeper available. 我們四處打電話詢問，但還是找不到管家。
call sb back	回電	I called my boss back but he was out. 我回電給我的老闆，但他外出了。
call sg off	取消	Jason called the seminar off because of the bad weather. Jason因為天氣不好而取消研討會。
calm down	冷靜	It's no big deal. Calm down. 這沒什麼大不了的。冷靜一下。
care for	喜歡	Care for a beer? 想來罐啤酒？
carry on	繼續	He likes to carry on with his story. 他喜歡繼續他的故事。
carry out	完成	They carried out their plan in two months. 他們在兩個月內完成了他們的計劃。
carried away	得意忘形	The team got carried away when they finally defeated their opponents. 當他們終於打敗對手的時候，他們興奮得意忘形。
cash in	換成現金	They cashed in their stocks and bonds. 他們兌現了股票和債券。
cheat on	劈腿欺騙感情	I don't date a girl who will cheat on me. 我不會交一個將欺騙我感情的女孩。

check in	入住飯店或登機	I am calling from Viva hotel. When will you check in? 我從Viva酒店打來。你什麼時候入住？
check out	1. 退房	They forgot to return the keys when they checked out. 他們退房時忘記還鑰匙。
	2. 檢查	The company checks out all new employees. 公司檢查所有新員工。
cheer sb up	讓某人開心	He made that face again to cheer me up. 他再次做那表情逗我開心。
come across	無意中發現	I came across these old photos I had taken in Africa. 我無意中發現在非洲拍攝的這些老照片。
count on	倚靠	I am counting on you, my son. 我靠你了，孩子。
dash down	快速寫下	Allen dashed down a memo and sent it to everybody. 艾倫快速寫下一個備忘錄，並發給大家。
dine out	外出吃飯	We dined out because we didn't want to cook. 我們外出吃飯因為我們不想煮。
do sg over	重做	Teacher asked the children to do their homework over. 老師要求孩子們重做功課。
do away with sg	丟掉	Please help me to do away with all these stuff. 請幫我丟掉所有這些東西。
do sg up	穿緊衣服	Do your coat up. It's snowing! 下雪了！包緊你的外套。

doze off	打瞌睡	It's the 2nd time he dozed off during her speech. 在她演講中他是第二次打瞌睡。
dress up	盛裝打扮	You don't have to dress up to attend this party. 你不必盛裝打扮參加這個聚會。
dress down	隨意穿著	The employees are allowed to dress down on Fridays. 員工可以在周五休閒穿著。
drop out	輟學	In this country, many poor kids dropped out of schools. 在這個國家，許多貧窮的孩子輟學。
eat in	在家吃	It will save us some money to eat in. 在家吃會讓我們節省一些錢。
eat out	吃外面	I don't feel like cooking tonight. Let's eat out. 我今晚不想做飯。我們吃外面。
end up	最終成為	He ended up becoming a teacher. 他最終成為一名老師。
fall for	1. 喜歡上	I fell for her the first time I saw her. 我第一次見到她就喜歡上她了。
	2. 被…騙	He fell for this hoax and gave them 200 bucks. 他被這個惡作劇所騙，給了他們200塊錢。
fathom out	理解	Human beings couldn't fathom out all the mysteries. 人類無法理解所有的奧秘。
figure sg out	搞懂	I need to figure out how to decrypt this message. 我需要弄清楚如何解密這訊息。

fight off	擊退	Our soldiers finally fought off the enemies. 我們的士兵終於擊退敵人。
fill in sg	填寫表格	Please fill in the immigration form. 請填寫移民表格。
fill out sg	填寫表格	Please fill out the application form. 請填寫申請表。
find out	發現	How can we find out his secrets? 我們怎麼能發現他的秘密？
fit in	融入	Sara didn't fit in with the other workers. 莎拉與其他工作人員無法融合相處。
focus on	焦點放在	This paper will focus on the company's strength. 本論文將焦點放在公司的優勢。
get along	相處得很好	My niece and my sister get along well. 我的侄女和我的妹妹相處得很好。
get away with	逃避處罰	Nobody can get away with cheating in this school. 沒有人可以在這所學校作弊而不被抓。
get back at sb	報復	Johnny got back at me for laughing at him. 強尼因我嘲笑他而報復我。
get back into sg	重拾興趣	I got back into that aerobic lesson. 我重拾對有氧課程的興趣。
get on sg	上交通工具	He waited for the children to get on the bus. 他等候孩子們上車。
get over sg	1. 從疾病中痊癒 2. 克服	Cindy finally got over the flu. 辛蒂的流感終於好了。 This country can't get over the inflation problem. 這個國家無法克服通貨膨脹問題。

get up	起床	I get up early almost every day. 我幾乎每天早起。
give in	讓步	At first he didn't want to help me, but he finally gave in. 起初他不想幫我，但他終於讓步了。
give out sg	發放	They were giving out coupons at the department store. 他們在百貨公司發放優惠券。
give up	放棄	Please don't give up. 請不要放棄。
go ahead	開始	You wanna taste this lobster? Please go ahead! 你想品嚐這個龍蝦嗎？開始吧！
go out with	和某人約會	Joan has been going out with Larry since last year. 從去年開始，瓊已經和賴瑞約會了。
go over sg	檢視	Please go over this report before you make a presentation. 在進行報告之前，請先檢視此報告。
go without sg	缺乏	They used to go without clean water. 他們過去缺乏乾淨的水。
hack into	駭入	He claimed that nobody could hack into this system. 他聲稱沒有人可以入侵這個系統。
hand in sg	遞交	I have to hand in my report by 9pm. 晚上9點前我必須遞交報告。
hand out sg	發放	We will hand out free copies in no time. 我們很快會發放免費的副本。
hang up	掛電話	He didn't say goodbye before he hung up. 他掛電話前沒有說再見。

hear from	聽到某人的消息	I haven't heard from Jack for a long long time. 我很久很久沒聽到傑克的消息。
hold on	稍待	Please hold on while I transfer your call. 在我轉接您的電話時請稍待。
keep on	繼續	Keep on dreaming! 繼續做夢！
keep sg from sb	不讓某人知道某事	Don always keeps the secret from everybody. 唐總是保守這個秘密不讓任何人知道。
knock it off	別鬧了	Would you knock it off? 你別鬧了好嗎？
lead to	導致	Good luck led to his success. 好運導致他的成功。
lighten up	放輕鬆	Lighten up while you still can. 趁你還能時放輕鬆。
log in/log on	登入	I can't log in to my email account. 我無法登入我的電子郵件帳號。
log out/log off	登出	If you don't log off somebody could get into your account. 如果您沒登出，有人可以進入您的帳戶。
look after	照顧	They took turn to look after their grand mother. 他們輪流照顧祖母。
look down on	低估	Never look down on anybody. 永遠不要低估任何人。
look for	尋找	Everyone is looking for love. 每個人都在尋找愛。
look forward to sg	期待	I'm looking forward to seeing you soon. 我期待著很快見到你。

make sg up	編造	Wilson made up a story about his childhood. 威爾遜編造了關於他童年的故事。
narrow down	縮小範圍	I am in a hurry. Please narrow the list down to ten. 我趕時間。請將名單縮小到十個。
nod off	打瞌睡	Grandpa nodded off while sitting in the armchair. 當爺爺坐在扶手椅上時在打瞌睡。
occur to	點子臨到某人	This brilliant idea occurred to me just in time. 我及時想到這個聰明的點子。
opt for	選擇	I opted for the white car. 我選擇了白色的車。
pass away	死亡	His father-in-law passed away last night. 他的岳父昨晚去世了。
pass out	暈倒	It was so hot in the zoo that an elderly lady passed out. 動物園裡太熱，一位老太太暈倒。
pass out sg	發送	Two girls passed out flyers on the street. 兩個女孩在街上發送傳單。
pass up sg	拒絕	I passed up the contract because I thought it's not fair. 我拒絕這合約，因我覺得不公平。
pay sb back	還	Thanks for lending me 300 bucks. I'll pay you back before Sunday. 感謝您借我300元。星期天以前我會還你。
pay for sg	付出代價	That thug will pay for what he has done. 那個惡棍會為他所做的付出代價。

pick out sg	挑選	I picked out these socks for you. 我為你挑了這些襪子。
point out	指出	I'll point out the mistake in this book. 我會指出這本書中的錯誤。
put sb down	羞辱	The press put the mayor down because of his policy. 新聞界因為市長的政策而羞辱他。
put sg off	延後	They are putting off the exhibition because of the typhoon. 他們因為颱風而延後展覽。
put out sg	撲滅	They helped the fireman to put out the fire. 他們幫助消防員撲滅火。
put sg together	組裝	You have to put the crib together. 你必須組裝嬰兒床。
put up with	忍受	I can't put up with this rowdy behavior. 我無法忍受這種粗暴的行為。
put sg on	穿上	He has put on his new jacket for the party. 他為派對穿上了新的外套。
run into	巧遇	I ran into my roommate in the park. 我在公園裡巧遇我的室友。
run over	1. 輾過 2. 複習	I didn't mean to run over your vase in the garden. 我不是故意在花園裡輾過你的花瓶。 Let's run over these handouts before exam. 在考試之前，先複習這些講義。
run away from home	翹家	The child ran away from home. 這孩子翹家。
run out	用完	We ran out of eggs so we couldn't make a cake. 我們用完了蛋，所以我們不能做蛋糕。

set sg up	安排	Our boss set a meeting up with the president of the company. 我們的老闆安排一場會議與公司總裁會面。
set sb up	陷害	My boss was set up by his competitor. 我的老闆被他的競爭對手陷害。
shop around	四處比價	I don't have time to shop around. 我沒有時間去四處比價。
show off	炫耀	He always shows off his new boots. 他總是炫耀他的新靴子。
sort sg out	解決	We have to sort this problem out before midnight. 我們必須在午夜之前解決這個問題。
stand by	支持	Don't worry. I will stand by you. 別擔心，我會支持你。
stand for	1. 字母代表意義 2. 容忍	ROC stands for Republic of China. ROC代表中華民國。 He's not gonna stand for it anymore. 他不再忍受它了。
stick to sg	堅持	You will succeed if you stick to the principles. 如果堅持原則，你會成功的。
sum up	總結	She summed up the main points in the lecture. 她總結了演講的要點。
switch sg off	關掉電器	Don't switch off the TV. It's my favorite show. 不要關掉電視機。這是我最喜歡的節目。
switch sg on	打開電器	He switched on his PC to download the new software. 他打開電腦下載新軟體。

take after sb	相像	George takes after his father. They are both tall and thin. 喬治相像他的父親。他們既高又瘦。
take off	起飛	My plane takes off in five minutes. 我的飛機在五分鐘內起飛。
tear sg up	撕	He tore up the letter then began to weep. 他撕了信然後開始哭泣。
think sg over	考慮	We need to think it over carefully. 我們需要仔細思考。
turn sg down	1. 降低音量 2. 拒絕	Please turn the TV down. It's already late. 請將電視機關小聲，已經晚了 I turned the offer down because I don't trust him. 我拒絕這邀請，因為我不相信他。
turn sg off	關掉電器	Please turn the lights off to save more money. 請關掉燈，節省更多的錢。
turn sg on	打開電器	It's 8pm. Let's turn the TV on to watch the news. 晚上8點了。讓我們打開電視看新聞。
turn sg up	增加音量	Can you turn the music up? 你可以把音樂調大聲嗎？
try sg on	試穿	May I try these jeans on? 我可以試穿這牛仔褲嗎？
try sg out	嘗試	Are you going to try this new machine out? 你要嘗試這台新機器嗎？
use sg up	用完	We have used all the milk up. 我們已經用完了所有的牛奶。
wake up	起床	She used to wake up at 4am each morning. 她以前每天早上凌晨4點起床。

warm up	熱身	Always warm up before you swim. 游泳之前務必熱身。
work on	研究發展	Scientists are working on this project. 科學家正在研究發展這個專案。
work out	1. 運動 健身 2. 成功	I work out three times a week. 我每週健身三次。 His plan didn't work out. 他的計劃不成功。
zoom in	放大檢視	If you zoom in, this picture might become vague. 如果放大檢視，這張照片可能會變得模糊。
zoom out	縮小檢視	If you want to see the whole picture, you might have to zoom out. 如果你想看到整個畫面，你可能需要縮小檢視。

常見成語

a penny saved is a penny earned
節省一分錢就是賺一分錢

Let's collect coupons. A penny saved is a penny earned.
讓我們收集優惠券。節省一分錢就是賺一分錢。

---

a picture paints a thousand words
一張圖抵過千言萬語

Use more photos in your slides. A picture paints a thousand words.
在幻燈片中使用更多照片。一張圖抵過千言萬語。

Achilles' heel
缺點

His Achilles' heel is lacking patience.
他的缺點是缺乏耐心。

---

actions speak louder than words
行動勝於雄辯

We should be voluntary workers first. Actions speak louder than words.
我們應該先成為志工。行動勝於雄辯。

---

all Greek to sb
無法理解

That senator talked about responsibility? It's all Greek to me.
那參議員談到責任？我無法理解。

---

appear out of nowhere
忽然出現

The leopard seemed to appear out of nowhere.
豹不知從哪冒出來。

● **apple of someone's eye**

眼中瞳仁----表示受到珍愛的人事物

This baby is his first child and the apple of his eye.

這個寶寶是他的第一個孩子，也是他最珍愛的。

● **around the clock**

日夜不停

That shopping mall is open around the clock.

那個商場全天候開放。

● **as fit as a fiddle**

健康良好

You are as fit as a fiddle.

你健康良好。

● **birds of a feather flock together**

物以類聚

Joseph is hanging out with Duncan again. Birds of a feather flock together!

約瑟再次和鄧肯混在一起。物以類聚！

● **beat around the bush**

旁敲側擊

Stop beating about the bush! Tell me what's really on your mind.

別再拐彎抹角，告訴我你真正在想什麼。

● **better late than never**

晚總比沒有好

I want to say sorry to her now. It's better late than never.

我現在想對她說抱歉。晚說總比不說好。

- **bite off more than you can chew**
  做超過你能力的事

Don't bite off more than you can chew. Let someone else do this work.
不要做超過你能力的事。讓別人做這個工作。

- **blessing in disguise**
  偽裝的祝福

His failure was actually a blessing in disguise.
他的失敗實際上是偽裝的祝福。

- **blood is thicker than water**
  血濃於水

He finally promoted his sister instead of Diane. After all, blood is thicker than water.
他最終提拔了他的姐姐，而不是黛安娜。畢竟，血濃於水。

- **bad blood**
  關係惡劣

There has been bad blood between the two families for years.
這兩個家庭多年來一直存在嫌隙。

- **behind someone's back**
  在人背後

It's impolite to talk about people behind their backs.
背後談論人是不禮貌的。

- **behind the times**
  落伍

These ideas are behind the times.
這些想法落伍了。

- **beside the point**
  偏離主題

Her comment was beside the point.
她的評論偏離主題。

- **bite your tongue(hold your tongue)**
  忍著不說

His behavior was really weird, but I held my tongue.
他的行為真的很奇怪，但我忍著不說。

- **black and blue**
  黑青

Lots of protesters were beaten black and blue.
許多抗議者被毆打到黑青。

- **break the ice**
  破冰(讓氣氛緩和輕鬆)

A nice smile can help people to break the ice.
一個微笑可以幫助人們破冰。

- **break the silence**
  打破沉默

A loud scream broke the silence.
一聲尖叫打破了沉默。

- **burn your bridges(burn your boats)**
  自斷後路

You're burning your bridges when you said that to your instructor.
當你對你的指導老師說那些話時，你正在自斷後路。

- **by the book**
  照章行事

Those people do everything by the book.
那些人做每件事都照章行事。

- **call it a day**
  今天到此為止

It's already 8pm. Let's call it a day!
已經晚上8點了。讓我們收工！

- **come in handy**
  派上用場

It's good to keep those tools. They might come in handy someday.
保留這些工具是好的。有一天他們可能會派上用場。

- **come to your senses**
  回復理性

David finally came to his senses and stopped drinking too much alcohol.
大衛終於回復理性，停止酗酒。

- **couch potato**
  懶惰蟲

Nelson has become a couch potato after he lost his job.
納爾遜失去工作後，已經成了懶惰蟲。

- **cross fingers**
  祝福

I will have a test tomorrow. Please cross your fingers for me.
明天我有個考試，請你為我祝福。

- **cry over spilt milk**
  後悔無益

Don't cry over spilt milk. You might have another chance.
後悔無益。你可能有另一個機會。

- **deep pockets**
  口袋深（有錢）

He has deep pockets. He likes to treat us to dinner.
他很有錢。他喜歡請我們吃飯。

● **do your best**
盡力而為

You will make it. Just do your best.
你能辦到的，只要盡力而為。

● **done deal**
已成定局

Don't worry. The contract is a done deal.
別擔心。合約已成定局。

● **don't count your chickens before they hatch**
別高興太早

Who knows the stock market will go up or down next week? Don't count your chickens before they hatch.
誰知道股市下週會漲或跌？別高興太早。

● **don't put all your eggs in one basket**
別將所有雞蛋放在同一個籃子----要注意分散風險

I have also applied for other jobs. I don't want to put all the eggs in one basket!
我也申請了其他工作。我不想把所有的希望只放在這個工作上！

● **down to earth**
務實的

Patrick is a dreamer. But his wife is pretty down to earth.
派翠克是一個夢想家。但是他的妻子相當務實。

● **easier said than done**
說的比做的容易

It's easier said than done to open a new branch office in this area.
在這個地區開設一個新的分公司，說的比做的容易。

● **eat your words**
收回所說的話

Jim said I'd never win, but now he has to eat his words.
吉姆說我永遠不會贏，但他現在必須把話吞進去。

- **enough is enough**
  適可而止

You have been a selfish partner for too long. Enough is enough.
你一直是個自私的伙伴很久了。該適可而止。

- **every cloud has a silver lining**
  黑暗中總有一線光明

Even though she fell in love with someone else, now you have more time to develop your own business. Every cloud has a silver lining.
即使她愛上別人，但現在你有更多的時間來開展自己的事業。黑暗中總有一線光明。

- **every dog has his day**
  每個人都有機會來臨時

Even he was finally granted the award. Every dog has his day.
就連他最後也獲獎。每個人都有得意時。

- **every now and then**
  偶而

I walk to my office every now and then.
我偶而走路上班。

- **fall from grace**
  失去別人的尊敬

I don't want to flatter my boss because it will make me fall from grace.
我不想奉承我的老闆，因為它會使我失去別人的尊敬。

- **fight fire with fire**
  以其人之道還治其人之身

Even though they have spread rumors about us, we don't want to fight fire with fire.
即使他們傳播了關於我們的謠言，我們也不想以其人之道還治其人之身。

- **fill somebody's shoes**
  取代某人的地位

Albert is such a great leader. It's almost impossible for Julian to fill his shoes.
阿爾伯特是如此偉大的領袖。朱利安幾乎不可能取代他的地位。

- **from now on**
  從現在開始

From now on, I am going to stop smoking.
從現在開始，我要戒菸了。

- **from rags to riches**
  鹹魚翻身

Ten years later that deliver boy became a CEO. It's another "from rags to riches" story.
十年後，送男孩變成為執行長。這是另一個 "鹹魚翻身"的故事。

- **from time to time**
  時不時

Since I live beside the lake. I go fishing from time to time.
因為我住在湖邊。我時不時去釣魚。

- **get up on the wrong side of the bed**
  吃錯藥

I don't believe you have made such a mistake. Did you get up on the wrong side of the bed?
我不相信你會犯這樣的錯誤。你吃錯藥了嗎？

- **get out of hand**

  無法控制

It has been 2 hours so the tourists are getting a little out of hand.
已經有2個小時了，所以遊客已經變得無法掌控了。

- **get to the bottom of sg**

  追根究底

We don't know what caused this problem. But we will get to the bottom of it.
我們不知道是什麼導致這個問題。但是我們會追根究底。

- **get wind of something**

  聽到風聲

Many people got wind of this scandal.
許多人聽到這個醜聞的風聲。

- **give me a hand**

  幫我忙

I can't carry this bag alone. Please give me a hand.
我無法單獨提這個袋子。請幫我。

- **give someone a piece of your mind**

  批評某人

Enough is enough! I'm going to give Steward a piece of my mind.
夠了！我要向史都華說出心中不滿。

- **good Samaritan**

  樂於助人的人

Caleb has always been a good Samaritan. Every year he donates 90% of his income to those in need.
迦勒一直是一個樂於助人的人。每年他將90%的收入捐給有需要的人。

- **hands are full**

  我很忙

Sorry, I can't help you. My hands are full.
對不起，我不能幫你，我很忙。

- **hang in there**

  別放棄

Hang in there! We can work it out.
別放棄！我們可以解決這個問題。

- **haste makes waste**

  吃快弄破碗

Don't rush the mechanic. Haste makes waste.
不要催促技工。欲速則不達。

- **head over heels**

  喜出望外

He sent me a flower yesterday. Now I'm head over heels.
他昨天給我送了一朵花。現在我喜出望外。

- **high five**

  擊掌慶賀

Leopards has swept Cougars! Let's high five!
豹隊橫掃了美洲獅隊！讓我們擊掌慶賀！

- **hold one's horses**

  耐心等待

Hold your horses and let her finish talking.
耐心點，讓她把話說完。

- **I owe you one**

  我欠你一個人情

Thanks for giving me a lift. I owe you one.
謝謝你載我一程。我欠你一個人情。

- **in a nutshell**

  簡而言之

In a nutshell, his problem is lacking experiences.
簡而言之，他的問題是缺乏經驗。

- **in a row**

  連續

They have won seven games in a row.
他們連續贏了七場比賽。

- **in the long run**

  長期而言

In the long run, who will win the final victory?
長期而言，誰能贏得最後的勝利？

- **it's not rocket science**

  沒那麼複雜

Just download that software one more time. It's not rocket science.
只需再次下載軟體。沒那麼複雜。

- **it is always darkest before the dawn**

  黎明前是最黑暗的

It is always darkest before the dawn. You will find a way out soon.
黎明前總是最黑暗的。你會很快找到出路。

- **it takes two to tango**

  要兩個人才能跳探戈(一個銅板敲不響)

It's not fair to blame it on him. It takes two to tango.
歸咎於他是不公平的。一個巴掌拍不響。

- **it's a piece of cake**

  太容易了

Decode this file? It's a piece of cake.
解碼這個文件？太容易了。

● **jump to conclusions**
驟下結論

Don't Jump to conclusions before you hear me out.
在你聽我說完前，別驟下結論。

● **keep an eye on**
看顧

Please keep an eye on my doggie. I will be back in 3 hours.
請看著我的小狗。我會在3個小時內回來。

● **keep a low profile**
保持低調

You'd better keep a low profile in the office.
你最好在辦公室裡保持低調。

● **keep sg in mind**
將某事記在心裡

Don't talk too much during the meeting. Keep my advice in mind.
在會議期間不要說太多話。記住我的建議。

● **keep track of**
追蹤

Kent always keeps track of the sports news.
肯特總是追蹤體育新聞。

● **keep one's word**
遵守諾言

He will keep his words.
他會遵守他的諾言。

● **lend sb a hand**
幫某人忙

Could you lend me a hand with these bags?
你能幫我提這些袋子嗎？

- **lend me your ear**

  請聽我說

Lend me your ear and I will tell you a secret.
請聽我說，我會告訴你一個秘密。

- **let bygones be bygones**

  讓過去成為過去

It's been one week after that argument. Let bygones be bygones.
這個爭論已經過了一個星期。讓過去成為過去。

- **let someone off the hook**

  讓某人脫離責任

Thanks for letting me off the hook. I am not good at painting.
謝謝你放我一馬。我不擅長畫畫。

- **lose face**

  失去面子

Try harder or you'll lose face.
更努力去嘗試，否則你會失去面子。

- **lose one's head**

  生氣

Vivian lost her head and shouted.
Vivian生氣了，也大喊。

- **lion's share**

  最大部分

Who received the lion's share of the profit?
誰獲得了利潤的最大部分？

- **long story short**

  長話短說

Long story short: Glen became his husband.
長話短說：格倫成了他的丈夫。

- **make ends meet**
  收支平衡

They have tried so hard just to make ends meet.
他們努力嘗試去達成收支平衡。

- **make hay while the sun shines**
  把握時機

He just returned to the office. Go ask him! Make hay while the sun shines.
他剛回到辦公室。去問他！要把握時機。

- **make up one's mind**
  決定

Stay home or move out? I can't make up my mind.
留在家裡或搬出去？我無法決定。

- **make yourself at home**
  當成自己家

Relax and watch TV. Just make yourself at home.
放鬆看電視。把這裡當成自己家。

- **meet sb half way**
  和某人妥協

I will meet you half way and give you 10% discount.
我會和你妥協，給你10％的折扣。

- **mind your own business**
  管好你自己的事情

What are you looking at? Mind your own business!
你在看什麼？管好你自己的事情！

---

never mind
沒關係

Never Mind. You can pay the money back next year.
沒關係。你可以明年再還錢。

---

night owl
夜貓子

Doctors said it's not healthy to be a night owl.
醫生說當夜貓子不健康。

---

never-never land
理想境地

This village is a never-never land to me.
這個村莊對我來說是一個理想境地。

---

no sweat
不麻煩

A: Thank you for helping me?

B: No sweat!

A：謝謝你幫我

B：不麻煩！

---

no way
不可能

You want me to break up with her? No way!
你要我跟她分手嗎？不可能！

---

now and then
偶而

We have dinner together now and then.
我們偶而在一起吃晚飯。

- **now or never**
  現在不把握以後沒機會

Christina will fly to France tomorrow. It's now or never.
克里斯蒂娜明天將飛往法國。現在不把握以後沒機會了。

- **on cloud nine**
  很快樂

I just got my promotion and raise. Now I'm on cloud nine.
我剛得到升遷和加薪。現在我很快樂。

- **on the same page**
  彼此同意

We need to hire more engineers. Are we on the same page?
我們需要聘請更多的工程師。我們彼此同意嗎？

- **once and for all**
  一勞永逸

I will solve my problem once and for all.
我會一勞永逸地解決我的問題。

- **out-of-date**
  過時的

Your hat is out-of-date!
你的帽子是過時的！

- **out of the blue**
  忽然間

Out of the blue, I received the invitation from him.
忽然間我收到了他的邀請。

- **out of the question**
  不可能的

Giving him a raise is out of the question.
給他加薪是不可能的。

● **peeping Tom**
偷窺狂

All the girls abhor that peeping Tom.
所有的女孩都憎惡那偷窺狂。

● **pull someone's leg**
開某人的玩笑

I was just pulling Paul's leg when I said his mom is coming.
當我說他的媽媽來了，我只是開保羅的玩笑。

● **practice makes perfect**
熟能生巧

Keep doing it! Practice makes perfect!
繼續做！熟能生巧！

● **pros and cons**
利弊得失

Nobody totally understood the pros and cons of investing in this new business.
沒有人完全理解投資這個新業務的利弊得失。

● **read between the lines**
了解隱藏的意義

If you can read between the lines, you will find he actually meant well.
如果你可以了解字裡行間的意義，你會發現他實際上是好意。

● **ring a bell**
讓人想起甚麼

Does the name "Wendy Smith" ring a bell?
"溫蒂史密斯"這名字是否讓你想起甚麼？

● **safe and sound**
安全無恙

We all came back home safe and sound.
我們都安全無恙回到家。

● **see eye to eye**
同意

They never see eye to eye on this issue.
他們在這事上意見從來不一致。

● **scapegoat**
代罪羔羊

That guy was a scapegoat.
那傢伙是代罪羔羊。

● **sit on the fence**
觀望

He had no idea which party will win the election. So he decided to sit on the fence.
他不知道哪一黨會贏得選舉。所以他決定觀望。

● **slip of the tongue**
說錯了

Did I say city zoo? It was a slip of the tongue.
我說城市動物園嗎？說錯了。

● **smell something fishy**
覺得事情可疑

Didn't you smell something fishy?
你不覺得事情有些可疑嗎？

● **so far so good**
目前為止還好

We have fixed the second problem. So far so good.
我們已經解決了第二個問題。到現在為止還挺好。

● **state-of-the-art**

Modern people like state-of-the-art technology.
現代人喜歡先進的科技。

● **tables are turned**
情況已轉好

My brother has become the supervisor. The tables are turned for me.
我的哥哥已經成為主管。情勢對我已轉好。

● **take a break**
休息

Let's take a 10-minute break.
讓我們休息１０分鐘。

● **take a rain check**
延後計畫改天再做

I won't go to movie with you tonight, but can I take a rain check?
今晚我不會和你一起去看電影，改天好嗎？

● **the last straw**
壓垮的最後一根稻草

For Lucas, that slander was the last straw.
對於盧卡斯來說，那誹謗是壓垮他的最後一根稻草。

● **think outside the box**
跳脫框架思考

Try to think outside the box. That new regulation might not be bad.
嘗試跳脫框架思考。那個新的規定可能不壞。

those who live in glass houses shouldn't throw stones
正人前先正己

Don't judge me for being late for work. Those who live in glass houses shouldn't throw stones.
不要因為我工作遲到而論斷我。刮別人鬍子前先把自己的刮乾淨。

---

through thick and thin
無論情況好壞

We have to achieve our goal through thick and thin.
無論情況好壞我們必須實現目標。

---

time after time
一次又一次

He warned us time after time.
他一次又一次地警告我們。

---

tip of the iceberg
冰山一角

That conflict is just the tip of the iceberg.
這場衝突只是冰山一角。

---

under the table
檯面下

The payment was under the table so he didn't have to pay tax.
付款是檯面下的，所以他不必繳稅。

---

ups and downs
高低起伏

Her life was full of ups and downs.
她的生活充滿了高低起伏。

- **user-friendly**

  對用戶友善

It is the most user-friendly interface I have ever seen.
這是我見過對用戶最友善的界面。

- **vice versa**

  反之亦然

Jack doesn't trust his boss, and vice versa.
傑克不信任他的老闆，反之亦然。（他的老闆也不信任他）

- **vicious circle**

  惡性循環

Don't let your life get into a vicious circle.
不要讓你的生活陷入惡性循環。

- **wash your hands of sg**

  不再涉入

Joy washed her hands of this investment.
喬依不再涉入這項投資。

- **waste your breath**

  浪費唇舌

He will never change. Don't waste your breath
他永遠不會改變。不要浪費唇舌。

- **with flying colors**

  高分通過

Mina passed the math test with flying colors.
米娜高分通過數學測試。

- **without a doubt**

  毫無疑問

Without a doubt, he will be our new mayor.
毫無疑問，他將是我們的新任市長。

● **you can't judge a book by its cover**
不要因一本書的封面而評斷(勿以貌取人)

She doesn't look very smart? Her IQ is 145! You can't judge a book by its cover.
她看起來不聰明嗎？她的智商145！勿以貌取人。

● **you reap what you sow**
種甚麼，收甚麼。

She doesn't want to help you now. You reap what you sow.
她現在不想幫你。你種甚麼，收甚麼。

● **your call**
由你決定

To do or not to do? It's your call.
做還是不做？由你決定。

● **you asked for it**
你自找的

You knew smoking was bad for your health. You asked for it!
你知道吸煙對你的健康有害。你自找的！

● **you bet**
當然

A: Do you want to join us?
B: You bet!
A：你想加入我們嗎？
B：當然！

● **you're telling me**
還用你來說

A: Wow! That guy is really gorgeous!
B: You're telling me!
A：哇！那傢伙真帥！
B：還用你來說？

● **zebra crossing**
斑馬線

Can you show me where the zebra crossing is?
你能告訴我斑馬線在哪嗎？

● **zero-sum game**
零和遊戲

Don't make it a zero sum game. Make it a win-win situation.
不要讓它成為零和遊戲。使其成為雙贏的局面。

● **zip it**
閉嘴

Kevin was about to say the wrong thing, so I told him to zip it.
凱文即將說錯話，所以我告訴他閉嘴。

英語工具書
16

最直覺的英文文法

雅致風靡　典藏文化

親愛的顧客您好，感謝您購買這本書。

為了提供您更好的服務品質，煩請填寫下列回函資料，您的支持是我們最大的動力。

您可以選擇傳真、掃描或用本公司準備的免郵回函寄回，謝謝。

姓名：	性別：　□男　□女
出生日期：　年　月　日	電話：
學歷：	職業：　□男　□女
E-mail：	
地址：□□□	
從何得知本書消息：□逛書店 □朋友推薦 □DM廣告 □網路雜誌	
購買本書動機：□封面 □書名 □排版 □內容 □價格便宜	
你對本書的意見： 內容：□滿意□尚可□待改進　編輯：□滿意□尚可□待改進 封面：□滿意□尚可□待改進　定價：□滿意□尚可□待改進	
其他建議：	

剪下後傳真、掃描或寄回至「22103新北市汐止區大同路3段194號9樓之1雅典文化收」

您可以使用以下方式將回函寄回。

您的回覆，是我們進步的最大動力，謝謝。

① 使用本公司準備的免郵回函寄回。

② 傳真電話：（02）8647-3660

③ 掃描圖檔寄到電子信箱：

yungjiuh@ms45.hinet.net

沿此線對折後寄回，謝謝。

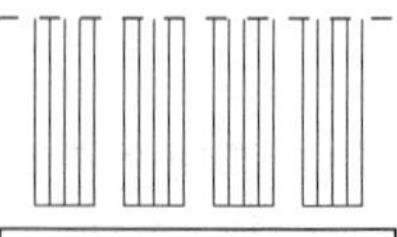

廣　告　回　信
基隆郵局登記證
基隆廣字第056號

221-03

雅典文化事業有限公司　收

新北市汐止區大同路三段194號9樓之1

雅致風靡　典藏文化

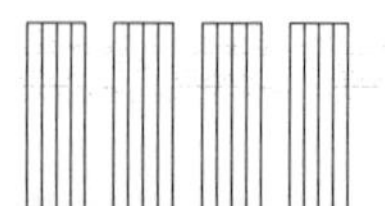